IRON MAN

MUTUALLY ASSURED DESTRUCTION

MARVEL

IRON MAN

MUTUALLY ASSURED DESTRUCTION

PAT SHAND

JOE BOOKS LTD

Published simultaneously in the United States and Canada
by Joe Books Ltd, 489 College Street, Toronto, ON M6G 1A5

www.joebooks.com

Library and Archives Canada Cataloguing in Publication
information is available upon request.

ISBN 978-1-77275-206-9 (print)
ISBN 978-1-77275-207-6 (ebook)

First Joe Books edition: July 2017

Printed and bound in Canada

1 3 5 7 9 10 8 6 4 2

To my mother, who gave me the most important thing in the world: stories.

CHAPTER ONE

The Shiniest Toy on the Block

"Your legend precedes you."

Luchino Nefaria conducted all negotiations the same way. When meeting a potential business partner for the first time, he would avoid making eye contact until he, Nefaria, had spoken first. It was an undetectable way of asserting control over an interaction from the very beginning, while maintaining the necessary façade of respect. That was the most important thing that Nefaria had learned in his years of working with men who aspired to be like him: give a man respect, and he'll make you *money*.

After a beat of silence, Nefaria finally raised his dark, deep-set eyes to meet the other man's gaze . . . if you could call the creature that sat across from him a man at all.

"*Henh*," the Ghost chuckled, a bitter and mirthless sound. "I could say the same about you, couldn't I?"

Nefaria surveyed the Ghost, who was draped over a chair that both men knew he didn't need. Every inch of the Ghost's body was covered in a battlesuit that glowed with a faint blue light, complete with a spherical helmet that obscured his face and made his voice into a hoarse, tinny echo. Nefaria had, of course, done his homework on the suit before inviting the man into his place of business.

The Ghost was a prodigious inventor—an artist by his own estimation—and the battlesuit was his *Mona Lisa*. It appeared to be a rather simple suit, a bit like an astronaut's or a deep-sea diver's, but, in truth, it was anything but simple. Glowing wires roped back from his breastplate toward his spine, and what appeared to be twin battery packs could be seen on either side of his chest. His helmet had two nozzles through which he spoke, though Nefaria remained uncertain whether the creature beneath the suit still had a mouth at all, or even a face.

Though he was unsure exactly *how* the suit did it, Nefaria knew that the battlesuit could make the Ghost himself or anything he touched completely intangible. The ability to move in and out of his corporeal form at will made him one of the most skilled assassins in the game. And while Nefaria had astounding powers of his own, he was self-aware enough to know that his team needed a specialized skill set for what he had planned. Indeed, impressive as the Ghost's phasing powers were, they weren't why Nefaria had called this meeting.

But before he could make his offer, niceties had to be exchanged.

"My men, did they offer you a beverage? I can have an espresso brought in, if you'd like," Nefaria said, looking down at the Ghost. "The finest you'll be able to find short of a trip to Italy, of course. Genuine."

"I'm good," the Ghost said, tapping on his helmet with his gloved knuckles. Snickering again, he leaned back in his seat. "I have to say . . . when I first got the call that you wanted to meet with me, I didn't think you'd be offering me the best espresso in Jersey."

"No?" Nefaria said. He saw his reflection peering back at him from the Ghost's helmet. Nefaria was a tall man with dark hair and a darker gaze, his skin tanned golden from years spent in the sun. He was handsome by anyone's estimation, and he knew it. It unnerved him to see his face warped before him.

"Nah," the Ghost replied. "Most of the time, when people call me to their *evil lairs of evil,* they end up threatening me. The whole 'never show your face in my city again' thing. I don't have what you'd call a 'good reputation.'"

"So I hear," Nefaria said. "My daughter once tasked you with killing a mutual annoyance of ours, and she was quite upset when you failed. I believe she'd still kill you, given the chance."

"Ah, Madame Masque. Good times. I kind of figured that's what *this* was about. Family vengeance, a real classic," the Ghost said, crossing his legs. "How *is* she doing, anyway?"

"You walked in here with the expectation that I would have you killed on my daughter's behalf?"

"That you'd try," the Ghost said, not even attempting to hide the glee in his voice. "I mean, your guys dragged me in here with a bag over my head and a device that jammed the signal from my battlesuit. What am I supposed to think?"

"I must take precautions, of course," Nefaria said. "You understand."

"Do I?"

Ignoring him, Nefaria pressed on, staring into the space on the bulbous helmet where he assumed the Ghost's eyes were. "Despite my methods, please know . . . no harm will come to you this day. Where my daughter and, I would assume, your other failed business partners differ is that they don't understand the kind of person you are . . . an idealist. A man of principle. They were seeking your services for something that would benefit them, and them alone. Am I correct?"

The Ghost assessed him for a second, cocking his head to the side. "Masque wanted me to kill Tony Stark," he said, and Nefaria noticed that the sarcastic edge to his voice had dulled. "And trust me, while I think that a world without Tony Stark would be a land of happiness and joy, his continued existence doesn't keep me up at night."

"That is exactly what I'm talking about," Nefaria said. He reached into his dark-mahogany desk and pulled out a red folder. He slid it across the table. "I want to make the world a better place for *all* of us."

The Ghost opened the folder with his clawed, gloved fingers and looked at the contents within. Giving him a minute to skim through the photographs and files, Nefaria sat back in his chair in silence, making a point to avoid looking at his distorted reflection. Finally, the Ghost uttered another oily chuckle.

"Nice little collection you've got there," the Ghost said. He did a double take as he flipped through the rest of the pictures. "Huh. Okay. Two questions. What *is* it, and how did you get your hands on these pictures? Because this . . . *henh*, this is the shiniest toy on the block, my friend."

"Don't pretend to be impressed, *my friend*," Nefaria said. "You and I both know that S.H.I.E.L.D.'s firewalls are vulnerable; my people took advantage of that. That's all. You could have done the same with about as much difficulty as it would take me send a text message. Security footage from a laboratory shouldn't impress a man of your standards."

"Yeah, well. Gotta give credit where it's deserved, don't I? Not everyone can do what I do. Besides it's not so much your people that impress me—though I'm sure they're all . . . you know . . . vaguely capable. It's that *thing* in the laboratory that's got me all types of intrigued."

Nodding, Nefaria strode over to the minibar on the side of the room, which was the only object in his cavernous office besides the bookshelves that lined the walls, his chairs and desk, and the pistol he kept inside of it. It was a long time since he'd needed to rely on such a weapon, but its cool weight reminded him of a life that seemed worlds away from the man he was now. Sometimes, he missed those times.

His back to the Ghost, Nefaria slowly poured himself a glass of water, making his guest wait as he took a sharp gulp. He wondered what would look back at him from behind broken glass if he reached into his desk for his pistol and then put a bullet into his own reflection on that ridiculous helmet. He chuckled to himself at the thought.

The Ghost waited.

Finally, amused by his own thoughts, Nefaria continued with a wormy grin, looking at the Ghost from across the room. "The fine men and women employed in my think tank are impressive, no doubt . . . without their help, I would've never managed to pull S.H.I.E.L.D.'s files. I would've never known S.H.I.E.L.D.'s newest and dirtiest little secret. Nor would I have learned that my people . . . their abilities have limits, Ghost. I know now that I need a more . . . specific type of talent for what comes next."

"Funny. This is sounding pretty much like something that would benefit *you*," the Ghost said. "Which, considering my rate for government espionage of this level, I can't say I mind. But let's be honest here. If I'm right about what I think those files mean, and let's not kid ourselves, I'm not often wrong . . . we're looking at a weapon of mass destruction. First guess? You want me to get it for you."

Nefaria frowned, waving off the Ghost's words as he would a fly buzzing around his head. "You're thinking on the surface. I've been told you're cleverer than that. *Listen* to me. I know you've had your run-ins with Stark. Have you met Captain America? The rest of the Avengers?"

"Some," the Ghost said. "Can't say that I'm a fan."

"Imagine again, if you will, that world without Iron Man," Nefaria said. "You say his existence doesn't bother you? Fine. Then imagine a world without Captain America, without the Hulk, without Thor, without Black Widow, without War Machine, the Falcon, Ant-Man, Spider-Man, Black Panther. . . . Think less about these people and more about what they stand for. Oppression. Limitations. Marginalization! Picture a world where men are left to thrive, without interference from people who have delusions of grandeur every bit as ridiculous as their costumes."

"You're talking about getting rid of the Avengers?" the Ghost said. "I mean, yeah, in theory, sign me up. There isn't much that's more infuriating than the idea of these lunatics running around, taking justice into their own hands. Taking—taking *due process* away from the people, right? Claiming to be heroes, but using—what, using the power of *lightning* to beat on some poor sap in a mask robbing a bank because he can't afford health insurance with his minimum-wage job? Or—or with me, right? They would protect and *have* protected corporations, evil—*truly* evil—corporations from *me*. They see anyone who doesn't fit in their system as someone they should stop, someone they should beat on. They don't see it's the system itself that's the real threat to this world."

Nefaria nodded and turned back to refill his glass so that the Ghost didn't see his smile. Nefaria's research on the Ghost told him that there was more to the man than the advanced technology in the battlesuit. The Ghost was a killer, and he wasn't above shedding blood for either money or vengeance, but he was also staunchly anticapitalist and would like nothing more than to see the corporate institutions that controlled the governments of the world topple and burn, burn, burn until nothing remained but ash.

His was a passion that Nefaria could use. A weapon, like any other.

Nefaria sat back down at the desk, across from the Ghost. "I do want you to steal that weapon. And once I have it, I can—*we* can—use it to take down not only the Avengers, but S.H.I.E.L.D. as well. I cannot keep my family safe and cared for with these organizations waiting for me to pop back up on the grid."

"Your family, huh?" the Ghost said with a smirk. He tapped the helmet where his nose would be. "*This thing of ours?*"

Nefaria didn't dignify him with a response.

The Ghost rolled his shoulders and leaned back in the chair. "All right then," he said. "So what's the plan?"

Nefaria smiled. "What is *your* plan? I'm offering you a great deal of money for a reason."

"I break into S.H.I.E.L.D., hack into this big hunk of whatever, and send it your way. Then?"

"Then, we can proceed one of two ways," Nefaria said. "If you are eager to part ways, I will shake your hand and you will leave my place of business with a briefcase. That briefcase will be loaded with ten million dollars. Just outside of this facility, there will be a private jet that will take you wherever you'd like to go. I hear that Cancún is beautiful this time of year."

"Or?"

"Or, you continue working for me, and the money continues to flow. I have big plans for this so-called weapon of mass destruction."

The Ghost cocked his head to the side. He looked, to Nefaria, like an alien. "Yeah?" the Ghost said. "What kind of plans?"

"We're going to take a page from our friend Mr. Tony Stark's book," Nefaria said, leaning in with a smile that didn't reach his eyes. "We're going to build a new future."

CHAPTER TWO

The Man, the Machine, and the Moustache

For a self-proclaimed futurist, Tony Stark had a stubborn habit of showing up late.

Presently, Tony was careening through the clear blue sky above one of his favorite places in the world—San Diego—in his newest armor. A scarlet and golden bullet to the beachgoers below, Tony indulged them (or, if he were being honest, indulged himself) by swooping down to the beach to wave at passing boats, flying alongside dogs chasing balls that their owners had thrown, and sending waves of cold water splashing down on the women on the beach who caught his eye.

Many women on the beach caught his eye.

Tony Stark was a genius inventor, a billionaire entrepreneur, a playboy savant, and, lest anyone forget, a philanthropist.

Also, he was Iron Man: a super hero.

Tony Stark hadn't always been the man he was now, though. His story had been told many times in countless

tabloids, documentaries, and unauthorized biographies—
Tony's favorite of which was titled *Tony Stark: The Man,
the Machine, and the Moustache.* His team of lawyers always
begged Tony to send these publishers cease and desist let-
ters, but if they stopped publishing ridiculous books about
him, what would he line the shelves of his otherwise empty
office with?

Either way, with or without *The Man, the Machine, and
the Moustache* and its like, everyone knew Iron Man's origin
story. Tony had been gifted in every sense of the word—
a boy genius who grew up to inherit his father's business
and wealth. When he first took over Stark Industries, Tony
was worlds away from what anyone would consider a hero.
His very public lifestyle of excess and luxury, paired with
unrivaled skills in his field, eventually led him into a very
bad situation: he was captured by a terrorist cell that ordered
him to create weapons exclusively for them. He said he'd
do it, and they'd watched over him as he labored. As Tony
worked in their dank and fetid laboratory, his mind racing
to figure out what in the world he could do to get out alive,
he realized that his captors were counting on his cowardice.

Why not surprise *them?* he remembered thinking.

It was there that Tony built his first Iron Man suit from
scraps and repurposed weapons. The suit saved his life then
and, if Tony were a sappy man, he might say that the Iron
Man armor had been continuing to do so ever since. On the

other hand, if he were a more self-aware man, he might add that the armor had also *gotten* him into a fair bit of trouble.

Case in point: this particular day in San Diego, as Tony idly cruised over the ocean, oblivious to the fact that there was somewhere he needed to be.

As Tony swooped low to the beach again, waving to a cheering little kid in Iron Man swimming trunks before rocketing past a perplexed pelican, a computerized voice spoke from within the suit.

"You're late, Mr. Stark," said F.R.I.D.A.Y., the artificial intelligence that helped Tony operate both his suit, as well as something far more complicated: his personal life. Her voice was cool and welcoming, though it had a slight undertone of contempt that Tony would never admit he appreciated. And yet, he did create her.

"You keep saying that," Tony replied, flying upward again.

"You programmed me to keep saying it," F.R.I.D.A.Y. countered. "Would you like to me play your recording? I can play your recording."

"No, no, we're good on the recording."

"You said you'd say that," F.R.I.D.A.Y. said. "Commencing playback."

"Who's in charge here?" Tony asked. "I said we're good on the—"

Tony was interrupted by his own voice. "Hey. Hey! Are you listening? If you're hearing this, this is now the third time you've dismissed F.R.I.D.A.Y.'s reminder. Third time! Which makes sense. You're—we're—insufferable about this kind of thing. We've got that whole '*I operate on my own schedule, who is my own AI to tell me what to do?*' thing going for us. And hey—I understand you. I get you. Us? Anyway, today isn't about you. Today is about *Pepper*. Remember? So quit shutting off F.R.I.D.A.Y.'s protocols and get where you need to be. I made a promise to a lady. Do me a favor, future me. Don't make me look like a jackass."

Tony winced, coming to a stop in midair. "That's right. That's right, that's right. Why didn't you say that in the first place, F.R.I.D.A.Y.?"

"I attempted to do so. Three times," F.R.I.D.A.Y. said. "Didn't you listen to the recording? I can play it again for you."

"Hey, question, did I program you to be this petulant? I don't remember programming you to be this petulant," Tony said. "So, we're late, and I've been hitting the snooze button. But I'm good on that now. We're doing this. It's Pepper time. How late are we?"

"Very late. Pepper's jet touches down in fifteen minutes."

"And this jet is touching down *where* now?"

F.R.I.D.A.Y. uttered an honest-to-goodness sigh. Tony made a mental note to take that function out of her programming, as it reminded him too much of . . . well, actually, almost everyone he'd ever spoken to for an extended period of time. "She is meeting you in the Bahamas, sir."

"I wasn't supposed to be on the jet with her, right? That would be bad. Very bad."

"No. You promised you'd meet her there."

"You know, this tone, you'd think I was out on a joyride," Tony said. "I was saving people. There were people in danger, and now they're saved."

"You stopped a casino robbery in Nevada three hours ago," F.R.I.D.A.Y. said. "In any event, *'in danger'* is rather hyperbolic. The casino was being held up by the Melter, of all people."

"And who am I to miss an encounter with the Melter? Always makes for a good story. And hey, listen, say what you want about the Melter, but he's stepping his game up. He actually did a little damage to the suit. Which, before I forget, that is something to work on while I'm . . . while I'm where again?"

"The Bahamas."

"Right, the Bahamas. Heat resistance. Extreme heat resistance. I'm talking major. I want to swim in a volcano without breaking a sweat. I don't want a Z-lister like the Melter making me look bad. We have the material? Enough to start on the basics without me?"

"Sir. Pepper."

"I know, I know!" Tony said. "I've had a stressful morning, all right? This is my sanity."

"You need to sleep more. If you slept more, you wouldn't need joyrides to keep sane."

"Again," Tony said, "not a joyride. There were distinct super heroics, Melter or not. How long will it take us to get to the Bahamas?"

"Just under an hour at Mach 3."

"An hour! You said Pepper gets there in fifteen minutes. Not good enough, F.R.I.D.A.Y. We have to give the impression that we didn't forget."

"We didn't forget. You forgot."

"Do me a favor—when I'm back in the lab, remind me to invent an AI with manners. You know, shining personality, endless optimism? Would you do that for me?"

"You won't get a rise out of me, Mr. Stark," F.R.I.D.A.Y. said. "What you will get is problem solving. Pepper's limo would normally take ten minutes to get from the airport to the resort. I can remotely misdirect her driver's GPS and delay their arrival by a half hour."

"Devious!" Tony said. "I love it. Cancel that last bit about inventing a nicer AI. You and I, F.R.I.D.A.Y., we're meant to be."

"Appreciated, sir."

Tony looking up at the clear blue sky, drinking in its vastness. He knew F.R.I.D.A.Y. was right—everything she was came from *him* after all, and of the many things Tony Stark was, incorrect wasn't often one of them. His mind was scattered and stressed, buzzing with ideas, and as freeing as it was to zoom around in the sky and relax for a moment, he needed some actual leisure time. He needed to be a person.

That was the hardest part of Iron Man—remembering that it was just part of him, and not the other way around.

"All right, F.R.I.D.A.Y.," he said. "Mach 3 it is."

Without another word, Tony blasted off in the direction of the Bahamas, leaving everyone at the beach looking up in amazement as he left the sound barrier in tatters in his wake.

"Here I come, Pepper," he whispered to himself as the ground below him became a stream of colors, a water-color image of blue and green and brown and red running together, blurring past him.

F.R.I.D.A.Y. knew well enough not to respond.

To a man like Tony Stark, there was nothing less relaxing than sitting still. However, as he reclined on the white sand at the Bahamas' best resort, the sun warming skin that it hadn't touched in weeks, Tony looked out at the clearest water he'd seen since his last ridiculously extravagant vacation and attempted to clear his mind.

No small feat, that.

During the ride, inspiration had hit and Tony's mind was still fast at work. He found himself, after seeing a terrier limping on the beach back in San Diego, cooking up a plan to manufacture affordable robotic implants for dogs—cats too, and maybe any kind of animal if he could figure it right (and, of course, he could). The specifics had been zipping around in his head ever since, from one beach to the next. He damn near had a blueprint.

But this isn't about you. Or that heat-resistant suit. Or that dog and its unfortunate limp, Tony told himself. *This is about Pepper Potts.*

He often wondered why Pepper put up with him during the times that she did. Throughout the years that Tony had known her, Pepper had been his secretary, his assistant, his boss, his confidant, his lover, and his best friend. Beyond that, she was perhaps the only person in the world who knew Tony's mind better than he did, and he found that his life was often better for her presence in it. Despite that, and despite the fact that she meant more to him than anyone, more than he could ever put in words, Tony spent more time tinkering in his lab—his church, as he called it—than he did with her.

These days, he knew that he would often let too much time lapse without even speaking to her. She never let on that it hurt her. After all, Pepper knew better than anyone that the price of knowing—truly knowing—Tony was that no matter how much she meant to him, no matter how much he promised to put her first, it was Iron Man that got the lion's share of Tony's time, his thoughts, and his care.

Any other way, and Tony might lose his grasp on sanity. They both knew that.

Even so, here Tony was, tanning on an empty beach as a baffled Pepper Potts walked toward him, lightly kicking up sand with each long stride.

Tony turned in her direction and lowered his sunglasses. Pepper was beautiful with her red hair pulled up in a pony-tail and her eyes scrunched in confusion as she looked around the beach, unable to comprehend what she was see-ing. Over her white and golden swimsuit, which Tony'd had waiting for her in their room upon check-in, Pepper wore a soft, white robe that flowed in the warm breeze, stretch-ing behind her like a cape. Tony couldn't wait until the sun brought out those freckles on her cheeks. He missed them during the winter. He missed them now.

Pepper stopped in front of her empty beach chair and looked down at Tony. Putting one hand on her hip, she used the other to gesture around their vacant paradise.

"Well?" she said.

"Well, I for one think it looks great," Tony said. "F.R.I.D.A.Y. was pushing for the pink, but to my eye, you're an absolute angel in white."

Pepper plopped her bag down and climbed into her beach chair, looking at Tony with wide, green eyes. "You didn't."

Tony narrowed his eyes, looking around at the beach as

if seeing it for the first time. "Oh!" he said. "I did. Yeah, I definitely did. Flight was okay? No turbulence?"

Pepper sank into her chair, rolling her eyes. "You're impossible. Absolutely impossible. You didn't have to do this . . . characteristically grand gesture. We could just be two people at a resort, like everyone else."

"We are two people at a resort. We're the *only* two people at this resort. Is it not romantic?"

"You rented out the *entire place*. That's a crazy-person idea, Tony," Pepper said. "Certifiable."

Tony pushed up his sunglasses and offered a wide grin. His glee was almost childlike.

Pepper sighed, but couldn't hide the smile growing on her lips. She took Tony's hand in hers.

For a moment, Tony's mind was quiet.

"It is romantic," Pepper said softly. "And still crazy. Next time, I wouldn't mind just being a tourist. Just one of the crowd. A regular person."

"There can still be a crowd," Tony said. "The entire staff is still here. Granted, the vast majority of them are probably playing around on their phones or something. For some reason, it's a slow day for them."

"You're impossible," Pepper repeated, but this time, she held Tony's hand even more tightly.

"So," Tony said. "What's on the docket? Here, we have the world's whitest sand and bluest water. Back at the resort, I'm pretty sure they mentioned that their pool goes on for—what was it, a mile? Mile and a half? Big pool. There's also a bar smack dab in the center of said pool, if you're going for a swim and decide that you're in the mood for—you know, a piña colada and getting lost in the rain. Personally, I'm not much into health food, but they have a great selection of champagne—"

Pepper laughed and leaned over her seat to rest her head on Tony's shoulder. "Hey. Tony?"

"Yes?"

"Stop talking for a second."

"Can do."

Together, they looked out at the water. Tony wondered if Pepper was thinking the same thing as he was, about how hard it was to find the divide between the sky and the ocean. Tony had never seen water like that, that blended into the sky so perfectly—or maybe he'd never taken the time to look.

Maybe, after all of that, this weekend actually *was* for the both of them.

Tony and Pepper enjoyed almost three full hours of peace, which Tony would later decide was probably some sort of record. They sunbathed for as long as Tony could sit still, talking a little but mostly enjoying each other's company.

Tony shared his idea for the canine prosthetic, which made Pepper laugh. He even whispered an order into his watch for F.R.I.D.A.Y. to put a patent on what he was tentatively calling "Next Step for Dogs" while Pepper was in the bathroom.

Then they swam in the warmest beach water that either of them could remember before moving to the pool, where they enjoyed drinks—a ginger ale for Tony and, indeed, a piña colada for Pepper—before heading to the spa for massages. Tony got, to quote Pepper, "a little twitchy" when the burly masseuse informed Tony that his back had the worst knots she'd ever felt.

"By far the worst," she'd said. "No contest."

"Yes, thank you. I have the worst back of all the backs."

"It's like an old, gnarled tree," she said, digging her elbow under his shoulder blade and moving it in circular motions. "No, it's like an old, gnarled tree wrapped around another old, gnarled tree."

"Great," Tony said, his voice pained. He thought he heard Pepper chortling, but her masseuse—who Tony noted seemed to have a distinctly lighter touch—was blocking his view of her face.

When the two of them left the spa wearing twin white, plushy robes, which Tony couldn't deny was perhaps his favorite attire not powered by repulsor tech in the world, they were greeted in the hallway by a familiar face. An incredibly stern, familiar face.

Tony pointed at the woman in front of them and shook his head. "No. No, nope. No, no."

Maria Hill, the director of the Strategic Hazard Intervention Espionage Logistics Directorate, or S.H.I.E.L.D., stood before Tony and Pepper in her black and white uniform, which Tony was beginning to suspect was the only outfit she owned. Her white combat boots brought her to Tony's height, but she still managed to somehow look down on him with her brown eyes. Hill and Tony had been through a lot together, much of which was Tony's fault. But still, an unexpected appearance from Maria Hill usually meant that Tony had to drop what he was doing for something that Hill deemed important.

"Hello, Maria," Pepper said, reaching out a hand.

Maria shook it. "Potts."

Hill began walking down the hall, and Pepper, baffled, followed her toward the lobby, forcing an exasperated Tony to go along.

"Why are we following her?" Tony hissed. "We could actually be doing the opposite of this right now."

"Just see what she wants," Pepper whispered back.

Hill came to a stop in the middle of the cavernous room and looked off to the side at the waterfall that created a sound that, in any other room, would've been tranquil. Yet, Tony could think of nothing less tranquil than a resort with no one in it besides himself, Pepper, Maria Hill, and the bewildered staff that hovered in the background.

Maria turned to Tony, offering him a sardonic grin. "Nice place, Stark. Kind of empty."

"You do have a way of clearing out a room," Tony said.

"Tony rented out the entire resort for the weekend. Just the two of us," Pepper said, her voice flat. Tony closed his eyes, breathing in sharply. He knew that tone, and it didn't bode well. Pepper knew exactly what a Maria Hill appearance meant, and he knew that there was no just "seeing what she wanted." Tony decided, right then, that he was not going to play along. Not this time.

"That's a very Tony Stark thing to do," Hill said, but Tony had already turned away from her.

"Listen up, wonderful staff members. I believe I booked my reservation—how long, a year ago?" Tony said, looking toward the hotel workers, who were huddled at the marble front desk, some of them indeed twiddling around on their phones. "I'm aware that her congress woman–inspired haircut suggests that she means business, so I understand the intimidation, but I don't remember inviting a third wheel. How about you show Director Hill out, offer her some complimentary mints, maybe, and we'll be on our way?"

Tony took Pepper's hand and began to turn around, but Pepper pulled him back. She smiled cordially at Hill, who seemed completely unbothered by Tony's remark.

"Pepper?" Tony said, still refusing to address Hill.

"Tony," Pepper said. And it was all she needed to say.

Tony slumped his shoulders and turned back around to look at Maria Hill, who stared at him from beneath arched eyebrows. "I don't want to be here, Stark. You're in a robe."

"I *am* in a robe," Tony said. "I was kinda hoping to stay in one."

"I think you'll change your mind," Hill said, pulling her cell phone off of her belt. Her fingers danced across the screen, which briefly illuminated her face in a dim, blue light before she passed the device to Tony.

Pepper leaned over Tony's shoulder as he looked at the screen.

It was live footage from inside S.H.I.E.L.D. headquarters. Tony fiddled around, swiping his fingers across the screen and zooming in. The app showed that there were four cameras set up in the lab, and Hill's phone allowed him to switch to the view of his choice. In this case, though, Tony wasn't quite sure where to start. The laboratory was big—far bigger than the main lab he'd seen when he'd last visited. A team of S.H.I.E.L.D. agents and lab workers, some of whom Tony recognized, were gathered around a thick, reinforced-glass tank. Some of them were operating devices that reached robotic hands into the tank while others took notes.

"That's a mighty big lab," Tony said. "Have you been hiding this from me? You know this is something I would've liked to see."

"Look at what's *inside* the lab," Hill said.

"What *is* that?" Pepper asked.

Tony touched his index finger and thumb to the center of the screen and then slowly spread them apart, zooming in to get a better look at the contents of the tank. A bright light was gleaming off of the object inside, so he switched to the camera opposite and did the same.

What appeared to be a twenty-foot-tall robot stood in the glass tank, its surface gleaming as if it had just been polished. At first, it appeared to be purely black, but as Tony moved to the camera angle across the room, and then switched to another, he caught tones of green, blue, and red in its luster. The robot was humanoid, much larger toward its cranial area than the legs, which were almost spindly. It reminded Tony of his own creation, the Hulkbuster armor, but upon further examination, those comparisons fell away. The figure looked utterly alien—like some kind of terrible, oversized beetle that stood on its hind legs as if poised to attack. It loomed to what seemed to Tony's eye to be at least twenty feet over the people in the lab, looking down at them from a gleaming, emerald visor. After another zoom, Tony could see that its armor was emblazoned with glyphs—some assortment of symbols that Tony, who had traveled not only the world but a good portion of space as well, couldn't recognize for the life of him.

What was most amazing to Tony was the fact that it was standing despite the massive core supported only by stick-like legs. Never mind the glyphs—its physical craftsmanship was unlike anything Tony Stark had ever seen.

"What is it?" Tony asked.

"That's what we're wondering," Maria Hill replied.

"I'm not sure if it's the most beautiful thing I've ever seen or a monstrosity," Tony said, narrowing his eyes and zooming in again. "It shouldn't . . . the *balance*! That thing should be tipping over, no matter how lightweight it is. This design doesn't make any sense."

"That's the consensus," Hill said. "And when something shows up on our doorstep and we can't figure out what it is or what it's meant to do, that's a problem."

"Yeah, yeah, of course," Tony said. He stared at the screen, lips parted, unaware that Hill was holding out her hand, waiting for him to hand back her phone.

Pepper nudged Tony, who looked up with a start, as if waking from a dream. Shaking it off, he gave the phone back to Hill, and nodded to himself, barely able to contain his excitement.

"I obviously have to see what that is. I . . ." He held up a hand, as if physically stopping himself from continuing that thought. He turned back to Pepper, who looked at him with tired eyes. "But . . . but, but—but that can wait. Pepper and I, we—we just got here, and we have the entire weekend planned. Me and Pepper."

Tony hoped that the words he was saying were forming

complete sentences. He couldn't get that robot—if that's what it was . . . what if it was an android, or a suit, or some kind of gigantic drone?—off of his mind for a second. What kind of man was he, he wondered, that he had the most beautiful, patient, and by all accounts fantastic, woman he'd ever met in an equally fantastic robe next to him, and all he could think about was a hunk of metal—*maybe* metal?—that looked like an oversized scarab?

Hill narrowed her eyes, pressing on. "Tony, this could be something huge. I hate to fuel your already staggering ego, but we've had our brightest and sharpest on this for days. We've made zero progress, and everyone who is anyone who has looked at it is unnerved. And that's putting it lightly. I need you on this, now."

"Just showed up on your doorstep, huh?" Tony said, arching a brow. "Where'd you find it?"

"Classified," Hill said.

"From me, even?" Tony asked, startled.

"And you need him now," Pepper repeated. "Why? If you've had this for days, why right now?"

"We have a very limited amount of time to crack into whatever this is before the Pentagon takes it for themselves," Hill said. "I've had to call in a lot of favors to keep this in my lab for as long as I have. I'd like to make sure it doesn't get confiscated on my watch, considering, for all we know, it could be an enemy weapon."

"So?" Tony asked. "I don't have any horse in your bureaucratic race."

"I'm well aware of that. However," Maria Hill said slowly, lifting her brows. "If you don't help us, you never *see* it."

"Oh," Tony said. "Well . . ."

"That's it, Stark. If you don't come," Hill continued, "it disappears. Which maybe isn't the worst thing in the world. But then . . . then, it's out of S.H.I.E.L.D.'s hands forever, and in the hands of people who will lock it away in the vault as if it never existed. *That* prevents S.H.I.E.L.D. from examining a possible threat."

Tony looked at Pepper, whose expression was blank. She already knew what he was going to do, and Tony was painfully aware of that.

"Once you assess what we have, we'll debrief you on how we uncovered the . . . item. Everything we know," Hill said, a note of impatience in her tone. She looked over Tony's shoulder and scowled at the hotel staff, who continued to eye them. Seemingly deciding that they couldn't hear her, Hill brought her voice to a whisper and looked Tony Stark right in the eye.

"The running theory," Hill whispered, "is that this item, whatever it is . . . is *not* from Earth."

* * *

As Tony zipped up his suitcase in their penthouse suite, he could feel Pepper's eyes boring a hole in his back. He held his bag, not wanting to turn around to meet her gaze.

"It's okay, Tony," she said, in a voice that suggested it was anything but. "If you had said no, I would've made you go."

"That's only because you know that if I stayed, I would've spent the rest of the vacation a million miles away," Tony said, looking out the window that overlooked the beach, which was empty and white, like rolling hills of sugar. He knew that it would only make things worse if he said it, but he'd had a good time.

He turned to Pepper and gave her a quick kiss on the cheek, never meeting her eyes. She lightly touched his arm as he walked past her.

"It's the right thing to do," Pepper said. "You know I know that."

"Better than anyone else," Tony said, walking toward the door.

"You wouldn't be you if you left them hanging," she said.

Tony grasped the knob and allowed himself a glance at Pepper over his shoulder. She was still in her robe, standing in front of the bed. He took in the crisp white sheets, clean and folded. Undisturbed. He wondered how long she'd stay at the resort after he left.

Not long, he suspected.

"I owe you one," Tony said, before opening the door and sliding out.

Now alone in the room, Pepper sat on the bed and stared at the spot where Tony Stark had stood moments before.

"I'll add it to your tab," she said.

CHAPTER THREE

First Contact

Less than an hour later, Tony Stark and Maria Hill walked side by side through the long, sterile halls of S.H.I.E.L.D.'s headquarters. With off-white walls at every turn and the smell of disinfectant in the air, the facility reminded Tony of two of his least favorite places: hospitals and his middle school, the former of which he visited far too often, and the latter of which he'd rather forget entirely.

They passed countless men and women who, as far Tony knew, could've been clones with their matching suits and sunglasses.

"The dress code is as strict as ever, I see," Tony said, giving a mock salute to a passing agent. Before leaving the resort, Tony had put on a pair of jeans and a thermal shirt, rolling the sleeves up over his tan arms, which made him stand out even more than he usually did in this sea of suit and ties at the S.H.I.E.L.D. headquarters. The only thing he had in common with the agents in the hall was that he also held a briefcase, but what it contained was far more spectacular than files, folders, and a bagged lunch. "There's a lot to be said about a casual Friday."

"Those are the first words you've said to me since we boarded the jet," Hill said. "I thought you were giving me the cold shoulder."

"That would be immature."

"Which is exactly what I was thinking," Hill countered. She stopped in front of a steel-reinforced set of double doors, then pressed her thumb on a glowing pad that was installed above the knob. The pad beeped twice and the doors opened inward with a hissing sound, leading into a small room with yet another set of doors in front of them. Hill motioned for Stark to hurry up and follow her inside.

He followed. "I should be back there with Pepper."

"Hands up," she said, stretching her own arms into the air. Tony followed suit as a series of green beams swept over them. "Pepper seemed to understand the urgency of the situation."

"She understands, yeah," Tony said, letting out a bitter chuckle as the green beams snapped off. "She understands better than anyone else."

Hill eyed Tony, then gestured to his briefcase. "What've you got in there? I thought for sure it would've set off the censors."

"It?" Tony asked, flashing a grin. "Not sure what you mean by '*it*.' I've just got some tools in here. Regular-person tools."

"Ah. So you've made it so it can't be scanned, huh?"

Tony shrugged. "Regular-person tools," he repeated.

"I'll let you pretend I believe that. And listen, about Pepper, don't be so hard on yourself," Hill said, motioning for Tony to proceed along with her. "You'll take a look at the item, tell us what we're dealing with so quick that it'll embarrass everyone in the lab, and then you'll rub it in a bit before getting out of here. Because that's what you do. Pepper knows where you really want to be."

"Sure she does," Tony said. "That's the problem."

The second set of doors slid open to an elevator, which the two of them entered silently. Tony stared at his reflection, stretched tall and thin in the metal panels, as the doors closed and the elevator began its descent. As they stood in silence, Tony wondered if he was the first outsider that S.H.I.E.L.D. had approached with this, and if they'd told anyone else about the thing that was in that laboratory waiting to be experimented on. There were other, more obvious choices to review otherworldly things, but Tony was an Avenger, which made him closer to S.H.I.E.L.D. than he cared to admit.

S.H.I.E.L.D.—much like Tony himself—had a strange relationship with the super-hero community; one that was at times akin to a partnership and at other times more antagonistic. S.H.I.E.L.D. was a huge government agency that acted in what it believed was the best interest of the

United States, but in Tony's experience, the people who were left to clean up the messes were more often than not people who *didn't* get paychecks stamped with the S.H.I.E.L.D. insignia.

There had been directors whom Tony would've blown off no matter how shiny a toy they dangled in front of him, but with Maria Hill, at least he knew the kind of person he was working with. She was an intrusive, condescending, obstinate, and wholly noble person who was, *because* of all of those qualities, to Tony's mind, the most qualified person to ever hold her rank.

He'd never tell her that, though. He got too much of a kick out of messing with her.

"What are you smirking about, Stark?" Hill asked.

Tony tilted his head to the side, his smile broadening. "Nice things. About you."

"Right," Hill said, rolling her eyes.

Finally, after what seemed like forever, the elevator doors opened on a balcony that overlooked the laboratory Tony had seen on Hill's phone earlier. The "item," as Hill had called it, was still there, but now the scientists and agents were looking up at Tony, who gazed down at the work space from behind the glass wall that separated them.

"Hoooooly moly," Tony said, staring down at it, his eyes wide and shining.

"Is that your expert diagnosis?" Hill asked.

He stepped in front of Hill and descended the stairs that led to the main area of the laboratory, moving with the energy of a kid rushing to his gifts under the tree on Christmas morning. People in white coats shook his hand and said things to him, but Tony was too mesmerized by the hulking robot to listen. He set his briefcase down on a lab table and strode over to the mysterious item. It loomed more than twenty-feet over them, encased within a protective dome of thick, layered glass.

It was even more dazzling in person than it had been on the screen. These days, there wasn't much in the way of technology that could mesmerize a man like Tony Stark, but this was nothing like the uninspired inventions that the people who aspired to be like Stark brought to show off at conventions. No, this was more than machinery. Tony looked at the robot—if that is what it was—and he saw *art*.

With every step he took, the lights of the laboratory caught a different color in the robot's hull. Cool cerulean, dazzling silver, glittering amethyst—and yet, somehow, also the deepest and purest black. It hurt Tony's head to look at it, and he wondered if he was staring at a color that the human brain wasn't equipped to see.

He looked down at the robot's spindly legs, which ended in points that barely touched the floor of the laboratory, giving the gargantuan creature the appearance of having dancer-like grace. Tony's first thought was that if someone gave the thing a push, it would come crashing down . . . but looking at how it stood, sturdy and still, he knew that thought was dead wrong. He wondered if the legs had been constructed from a much denser, heavier material than the core, which would almost explain how it stayed standing, but even the way that it only touched the floor with the spear-point bottoms of its legs suggested exactly what he'd thought when he looked at the footage on Hill's phone: that the robot had no business balancing the way it did.

Its arms—the best word for the things that extended from its core, though Tony tried to stop himself from anthropomorphizing the thing—ended in serrated metallic claws that seemed designed to kill, as did the blades that extended from its elbow joints.

On the top of its voluminous core, which took up a great deal of its mass, sat a head—a helmet?—that was featureless except for a crystal, smooth and clear, that ran across its center like a visor. Tony squinted, trying to peer into the visor, but the robot just stared back, the dark, crystalline visor blank and empty. He wasn't sure what he expected to see, but he felt compelled to look the thing in its "eyes," as it were.

He waited until the chatter died down and the room was filled with a tense silence before snapping out of his reverie. It was at that moment, when he realized the entire room was staring at him, that he discovered that his heart was racing.

He chuckled at himself before turning away from the item to address the others. For a moment there, he'd forgotten there *were* other people in the room.

"You. You seem in charge. You have a clipboard," Tony said, addressing a tall, bald scientist. Before the man could stammer out a response, Tony gesticulated toward the protective glass casing around the robot, nervous energy twitching through his veins. "Let's get it out of there."

The bald scientist put the clipboard down and spoke to Tony, his eyes wide and just bloodshot enough to show that he'd been working for a long, long time. Tony instantly liked him. "Sir—Mr. Stark, we can't just—"

Tony grinned at him and held out a hand. "Call me Tony. Did we shake hands already? Eh, who cares, let's give it another go."

The scientist grasped Tony's hand. "Gil-Gilbert," the man said. His voice was a staccato of stammers and shakiness that comforted Tony. He knew the type; he'd worked with them since before college. This was a man who lived off of inspiration, caffeine, and a diet of ramen noodles that were always still a little crunchy—a workaholic who basically didn't exist outside of the lab. And Tony respected that.

"Gil," Tony said, turning back to the robot and putting an arm around Gilbert's shoulders. "I don't want to come in here and steal your thing. Clearly, you've been working hard. I hear you need help, though, and I'm here for that.

Thing is, we're not going to get anywhere if we're behind a glass wall."

"S.H.I.E.L.D. protocol says we can't, Mr. Sta—er, Tony," Gilbert said. "There's the obvious danger factor. This is a completely foreign object and, uh—just looking at it, obviously it's capable of being used as a weapon."

"Agreed," Tony said. "Which, hey, by the way—where *did* you guys find this thing? That's going to have to be square one here."

"Classified," Hill chimed in.

Tony spread his arms in exasperation, but kept his gaze on Gil. "She's talking *agent*. I don't speak agent. You and I, we speak the same language, Gil. Talk to me. What's with the glass case?"

"It has been . . . limiting. But because we don't recognize any of the tech, extra precautions must be taken. Hence the glass."

"Hence the glass," Tony repeated, nodding. He spun around, pointing to Hill. "Oh, mighty Director Hill. You did say you'd spill the beans on where you found this 'item.' Which, I'll say it again, I'm still waiting on that exposition, classified as it may be. How about some info? Just to start us off?"

"In time, Tony," Hill said. "I have to go through the proper channels to get approval. You know that. You'll know everything you need to know when you—"

"Riiiight, when I need to know it. Right. How about this? Let's compromise. What do you say you override protocol here and give these fine, hardworking ladies and gentlemen the go-ahead to pop this sucker out of its box. Gilbert has been working hard. Give Gil a break here."

Maria looked at Tony, deadpan.

"Because look," Tony said, rapping his knuckles on the glass casing. "If this thing really turns out to be a problem . . . this glass? It isn't going to hold it in. And, correct me if I'm wrong, we're a good mile underground, right? *That's* going to go a longer way toward containing this thing than this box."

"That case is made of material that could stop a close-range blast from a bazooka, Stark," Hill said. "I think it best we—"

Ignoring her, Tony tapped his index finger against the touch screen of the device strapped to his left wrist. To the layman—and, compared to Tony Stark, everyone was a layman—it appeared to be a watch. A watch that would, to be fair, bankrupt a middle-class family, but a watch nonetheless. But this watch was a little different.

A golden undersheath formed over his hand a split second before plates came out of the watch and covered his fingers, his hand, and then his wrist, forming the gauntlet from his Iron Man suit. Before Hill could finish her thought, he hit the thick glass casing with a left hook, watching with satisfaction as a deep crack spread through the many layers of the protective barrier.

He turned, grinning from ear to ear, to a stunned Maria Hill.

"That . . . is S.H.I.E.L.D. property," Hill said. Tony couldn't tell if she was aghast or impressed, so he chose to assume the latter.

"And it wasn't really doing much but setting your heart at ease," Tony said, tracing a finger along the cracks. "Two more lefts—and note that I'm a righty—and I'll be on the other side of this glass. If our rock 'em sock 'em robot here is really a problem, that case won't be any more effective than caution tape. I could punch it a little more if you need me to."

"I knew it," Hill said, pointing to his watch. "You haven't ever in your life cared what time it is. You brought your suit."

"Of course I brought my suit," Tony said, holding out his gauntlet with a wide smile. He tapped on his briefcase with his knuckles. "Because you know what? If we start tinkering with that thing, and it turns out you're right? And your 'item' in there is a problem? Iron Man can do a lot more to put it back down than a wall of broken glass. But something tells me you knew that."

Maria surveyed Tony for a long moment, her expression characteristically unreadable. "Go ahead," she said at last, walking past Gilbert on her way to the exit. "Retract the protective casing. And someone please make sure that we bill Stark Industries for the property damage."

"Okay, good," Tony said. "I'm on it. I'll have them buzz you if we need anything, Hill."

As she walked out of the lab, Tony caught the slightest smile tug at the corner of her lips before she disappeared from sight.

"Can I get you anything?" asked a younger scientist whose hair was shiny with gel he hadn't seemed to have gotten the hang of using.

"Coffee. Lots of coffee. Black. Just bring the whole pot," Tony said, eagerly watching as the protective dome slid away, one part of it lowering into the ground and another part lifting up into the ceiling. "And maybe some ramen noodles."

There was a ghost in the walls of S.H.I.E.L.D.'s headquarters, and not a soul in the building knew it.

Just as he had promised Luchino Nefaria, the Ghost was able to evade S.H.I.E.L.D.'s vast and intricate security systems without incident. He had phased through solid ground a few miles away from the facility as he floated insubstantially through miles of dirt and then, finally, cement, following the call of S.H.I.E.L.D.'s various server signals. When he was physically within the facility, he willed himself to drift up through the walls of the building until he felt a strange buzz in the base of his neck.

His battlesuit was designed to confuse S.H.I.E.L.D.'s laser

scanners enough to allow him to pass through any room in the building, from the overcrowded cafeteria to the vault with the highest clearance level, without being detected. The same technology made him invisible to security cameras when he had his power inhibitors activated, as he did now, but he still avoided walking in the open hallways, opting to instead phase through the maze of walls and ventilation systems that snaked through the building.

His Ghost-tech allowed for all of this, because—unlike Iron Man—he was no longer physically or mentally independent of his suit. The suit acted according to his will because his technology was so bound to his consciousness that there was no separating the two. Where he would've once had to program his suit to follow specific directions, now all he had to do was think *up,* and *up* he went. It was only the power inhibitors on his wrist that needed to be physically switched on and off.

Beyond his command over the suit's movement and physicality, the Ghost now heard what others didn't. To him, each piece of machinery he'd ever encountered had its own specific voice. It was his battlesuit that allowed him to hack past a firewall and override a machine's or a network's settings, but since fusing his mind with his Ghost-tech, he found that communicating with machines wasn't as simple a process as "hacking," though men like Nefaria would never be able to understand that. The Ghost didn't just tell machines what to do—he spoke to them, and they spoke back. He may not have heard voices in the traditional sense, but, after all, the Ghost had long since moved beyond the traditional idea of what a person was—a living person, anyway. Now, as he listened to the cacophony of S.H.I.E.L.D.'s many interwoven networks, he attempted to listen for a singular voice—a voice unlike any other.

That would be his target.

As the Ghost floated within the walls of S.H.I.E.L.D., he sifted through the many voices of the networks and machines on the premises, listening to one and then moving to the next. The encrypted Wi-Fi signals were a constant, hurried stream of voices that came together in a melodic hum. It was everywhere, always. That sound had become the closest thing the Ghost knew to silence.

The weapons in the building spoke in booming, harsh tones. The Ghost entertained the idea of hacking into S.H.I.E.L.D.'s system to launch a couple of missiles at his own enemies, just for something to do while he searched for the right voice, but decided against it. He had a mission, after all.

Would've been fun, though, he thought to himself, letting out a nasty giggle.

He followed the buzz that continued to drill into the base of his neck, and that was now spreading through his jaw and down his spine.

"Hello, there," the Ghost whispered. "Powerful, aren't you?"

The buzz picked up in pitch, and now a screeching whine like metal being ripped cut through the Ghost's battlesuit. The Ghost followed the signal, floating through the wall and into an elevator shaft. He held out his gloved hands and allowed himself to become corporeal as he felt the buzz grow stronger, telling him that he was getting closer. His feet touched down on a steel beam. He preferred to anchor himself physically when he used his Ghost-tech to remotely breach powerful security systems—it was an odd feeling, very much like his mind was drifting away from him, free-falling into a world of electricity and code, into a spinning vortex of 0s and 1s into which he could so easily lose himself.

Sometimes, he wondered if it would be peaceful to let go.

The Ghost shook off the thought, grabbed the steel beam to his side, and willed the components in his suit to reach out to the strange, alien buzzing.

An hour into his inspection of the mysterious robot, the once pristine laboratory had begun to adopt the chaos of Tony's home workshop. Spilled coffee had already made an impressive number of the tabletops sticky, tools had been strewn about, and—thankfully—all of the other scientists and agents finally got the hint that Tony was too polite to voice. Or, rather, that Tony was too wrapped up in his examination to voice. That hint, of course, was that the only way this would get done was if Tony and this beautiful, insane bit of craftsmanship were left alone. A few still watched from the balcony, but as long as his space was *his* space, Tony was aces.

The only problem was that he still had no idea what in the world he was looking at.

The gleaming material that the robot was made up of was completely unfamiliar to Tony—and that was a first. It had a smooth, deceptively soft finish, like plastic or cast iron. However, nothing Tony tried could even leave a scratch on its surface. The material didn't behave like iron, chromium, steel, silicon, Adamantium, or Vibranium. It was something *new.*

After using S.H.I.E.L.D.'s cranes to lay the robot on its back, Tony was able to bend the arms and the legs at the joints and, when he reached into the partition between the neck and the shoulder plates, found that its head spun around 360 degrees in response. Beyond that, the thing didn't move. He'd thus far come to the same conclusion as anyone else who had examined the thing thus far: it could be a robot, it could be a suit of armor in the same vein as his own, it could have a power source somewhere within its machinery, it could be operated remotely through some kind of third-party network, it could be a drone, it could be Russian, it could be Antarctican, it could be from Mars, it could be from an alternate reality, or it could be from a dimension where talking pigs ate bacon made from people. It could be *anything* from *anywhere.*

This, Tony knew, was frustrating to the men and women who had been working on this for hours. But not to Tony.

He was having the time of his life.

To Tony Stark, there were three categories of inventors. First, there were the people who wanted to add something of their own to the world—something new that no one else had ever thought of before. They wanted to build their own empires; wanted their names to be remembered.

Most of the folks in Tony's field fit in that group. Tony himself had once felt that way.

Second, there were those who used their best ideas not to build, but to destroy. Tony had met far too many of these for his liking, and found that those from the other groups who hadn't found success were too often wooed by the temptations that this ideology had to offer. Building is difficult; tearing down is as simple as it gets. Tony wished he didn't, but he understood that.

Third, there were the people who looked at the world and saw something missing—an essential piece that should have always been there but that had somehow been left out in an egregious error. It was their job, as the inventor, to fill that hole with the missing piece. Every idea, every project, every drop of sweat put toward their craft was done in service of finding that unknowable thing that would make the world a better place.

That was Tony Stark.

As Tony continued his attempt to break into the robot's hull, he couldn't help wonder what type of inventor had made the thing before him. As he worked, he felt its empty, obsidian eyes staring off into the nothingness. There was nothing in the robot's design that seemed more malicious than anything he himself had ever built, but he couldn't shake the feeling that whoever had created this thing was quite certainly *not* interested in building.

No, this was a weapon. Tony Stark knew weapons.

"There!" the Ghost rasped, as he felt the whining buzz crescendo. Whatever was powering this thing was completely unfamiliar to him, so he wasn't sure if he'd truly breached its system or just its first line of defense, but it was something.

Beyond having a voice, all systems have languages, and this one was different from anything he'd ever heard. As his tech explored the source of the buzzing, the Ghost felt as if his mind were racing through a dark tunnel. At the end of the tunnel was a dull, shining light that sometimes appeared to be blue, sometimes green, sometimes red. Every time he got closer, the tunnel shifted and he was racing again, ever moving toward his goal.

"Come on," the Ghost urged. It had been a long time since the Ghost had felt out of his depth, and the realization that the robot's system was fighting back in a way that was alien to every other network the Ghost had ever broken into before unnerved him. The system was behaving as if it were alive. As he pushed on, his vision filled with the fleeing light, he suddenly felt the buzz lash out at him. But instead of vibrating his bones within the suit, the light expanded and the buzzing grew hot. He wasn't sure if it was a physical attack or if the robot's tech was attacking his Ghost-tech—he had never *felt* a network assault him like this.

"There we go," the Ghost said, pushing further. "Give me your best shot."

The light, no longer fleeing, shot toward the Ghost. He felt it pushing against his tech, attempting to strip the battlesuit of its defenses. The force of it was so powerful that the Ghost feared that if he let up for even a moment, the robot's security system—if that's what this was—would not only kick him out, but would leave his own suit powerless, leaving him stranded in the S.H.I.E.L.D. elevator shaft, suffocating as the suit's oxygen supplies were cut off.

But he couldn't back out now. He'd already jumped off the cliff. Now, all he could do was stick the landing.

The Ghost laughed. "I'm not going out like that," he said. "Give . . . UP!" Instead of avoiding the light that was rushing at him, he closed his eyes and trusted his Ghost-tech, taking the full brunt of the attack head on. It would either kill him or his tech would topple the defenses. It had been a long time since death had scared the Ghost.

The Ghost's vision filled with a blast of blue flames as the light enveloped him. He felt his spine convulse and thought for a moment that he was having a seizure, but both the light and the pain were gone as soon as they came. The Ghost opened his eyes and found himself in the elevator shaft, clutching the steel beam tightly.

The buzz no longer surrounded the Ghost. Now, he *was* the buzz, vibrating in his own battlesuit with the foreign energy of the robot in the other room.

He was no longer alone. He was *in*.

He felt something straining to move, as if it was coming out of a long idle state. Closing his eyes, the Ghost willed his tech to push further, and then, suddenly, he could see— not through his own eyes, but through the crystal that was embedded in the robot's mask.

The Ghost's physical body remained in the battlesuit, slumped over in the elevator shaft, but his mind's eye was looking through the robot's visor at Tony Stark, who leaned over the hull with a sweaty brow.

The Ghost tried to raise the robot's arm to grab Tony's neck, but it was no good. It was still struggling to regain— *regain, what, consciousness?* the Ghost thought—and remained immobile.

The Ghost cleared his mind, focusing on forcing his consciousness further into the robot's system. Perhaps then he could force it to move. He began to hear clicks and chirps and a distant boom rising from the buzz.

"Yes, there you go," the Ghost urged. "Wake up. Wake up. We're gonna have some *fun*. Do you hear me?"

The Ghost jolted when he felt a cold burst of static in his skull, as if someone had poured ice water into his helmet. For a moment, as the strange energy shot through his body, he found himself shifting back and forth from his corporeal body to his ghost form, over and over. Warm static shot up his body and, now fully incorporeal, he began to float into the air, confused and on the verge of panic as he realized what was happening.

He'd reached out to the robot's mind. Now, whatever powered it was reaching back. Finally.

"Hello, there," the Ghost said, struggling to stay calm as he floated helplessly. "What's your name?"

Tony jumped down from the step stool, throwing a handheld laser blade off to the side as he walked away from the robot. The blade hit the floor with a sharp crack and Tony winced. He'd forgotten he wasn't in his own lab.

He looked up at the scientists on the balcony sheepishly. "Have Hill shoot me a bill for that one, too."

He wasn't going to give up until he was able to find out what made the item tick—if it did still tick, or if it ever did—but he was beginning to suspect that he wouldn't do so by breaking into its hull.

He'd tasked F.R.I.D.A.Y. with operating a nanodrone that was now examining the crevices of the robot and scanning it for any signals or interior machinery that could give them a clue as to what this thing's deal was.

"Anything, F.R.I.?" Tony asked.

"Unable to read its system, unable to hack into any network it might've been connected to, unable to get a 3-D scan of the interior—"

"Unable across the board," Tony said, sighing. "Keep at it."

As F.R.I.D.A.Y. continued her work, Tony waved to Gilbert, who was among the others on the balcony.

"Gil! Hey Gil, buddy!" Tony called.

Gilbert stared at Tony from the balcony like an excited puppy.

"Get Director Hill back in here, would you?" Tony shouted up at him. "She said it's *classified,* where she found this thing, but she can't expect me to give her answers if I don't know where it came from. I need her to drop the S.H.I.E.L.D. procedure bull and cut to the chase, okay? Tell her that, exactly. Verbatim. And then give her a patronizing wink, she really likes those."

A green light washed over the room from behind Tony, casting his shadow dark and tall across the floor. Thinking that he'd mistakenly triggered some sort of alarm, he turned around and looked up, shocked to see the robot, its visor glowing with brilliant emerald light, standing to its full height. Its limbs creaked and groaned as it stood on those pointed legs and surveyed the room with its glowing eye. Steam poured out of its joints, and its claws opened and closed, over and over.

"We have activity, sir!" F.R.I.D.A.Y. said. "Its systems are still unidentified, but they are most certainly active!"

"Perceptive," Tony said, balking at the robot. At its full height, it cast a shadow over the entire room, and Tony found himself standing in it.

He circled around it, as its head turned to follow him. He wasn't sure what was watching him through that visor, so he wanted to show that he wasn't going to attempt an attack.

Even though he had been attempting to cut it open with a laser just moments prior.

An impossibly deep voice boomed from the core of the robot, but Tony didn't understand what it said. Tony knew many languages, but this one was unfamiliar.

"Language undetected," F.R.I.D.A.Y. confirmed.

"Uh, sorry," Tony said, folding his arms as he spoke to the robot, ignoring F.R.I.D.A.Y. He kept his finger right above the screen of his watch, ready to act at any moment. "English?"

"Hello, there," the robot said, but this time, it spoke in another voice. A strange, distant echo of a voice that Tony vaguely recognized, though he couldn't place his finger on why. *That* was curious. The robot spoke again: "What's your name?"

"Tony. Tony Stark," Tony said, attempting to conceal his bafflement. "Good. First contact. I . . ."

There was an extended pause. Then, the original voice boomed once again from the robot, which took a menacing step toward Tony. Looming over him, its emerald eye flashing, the robot bellowed in its original voice, but now in English:

"I . . . am . . . Necrosis."

CHAPTER FOUR

The Result of War

"I . . . am . . . Necrosis."

The booming, inhuman voice vibrated through the Ghost's battlesuit like a surge of electricity. Just like that, he was back entirely in his own body—and no longer intangible. Stunned by the sudden pull of gravity, the Ghost let out a startled cry as he found himself free-falling down the elevator shaft. Before he had time to think himself intangible once again, he crashed into a hard beam of steel.

It had been a very long time since the Ghost had felt true bodily pain.

Crumpled on the beam, the Ghost looked down to see where he would've fallen had he not crashed. The shaft extended down farther than he could see. The fall would've killed him. He was sure of it.

The Ghost pushed himself up to his feet and stepped carefully across the beam until he could grab the wall. He still felt Necrosis's network in his mind—a warbling, unstable whine that made his teeth ache.

"Did you do that to me?" the Ghost hissed.

Silence.

"I *said*," the Ghost said, bringing his voice up to a venomous shout. "Did *you* do that to me?"

Silence again.

The Ghost balled his hands into fists. He'd never—*never*—felt a system like this. He'd broken through the weapon's firewalls, trumped its defenses, and taken over . . . or so he'd thought. It made no sense; even though the code was foreign, it was still code. The battlesuit had interpreted it and reconfigured it, as it had tens of thousands of systems before. If all was right in the world and dogs still barked and the sky was still topside, the Ghost should have had full control over this thing, this "Necrosis"—but he just didn't. He could sense it, but was cut off. Even artificial intelligence, if that's what he was dealing with, shouldn't behave like that.

It had gotten the best of him. He was seething, his helmet fogging up from his fury.

The Ghost grabbed his wrist and twisted the cuff of his battlesuit, undoing one of his signal inhibitors. He felt a rush of electricity surge within his suit as his power rose to 75 percent capacity. This risked making him detectable to S.H.I.E.L.D.'s security systems, but he didn't care anymore—he needed the extra power to completely infiltrate Necrosis's network. If Necrosis was trying kick him out of its system, it was time for the Ghost to take the gloves off and show this thing what his tech could really do.

The Ghost raised his hand, preparing to become intangible once again as his suit gleamed with energy. He waited . . . and waited . . . and waited.

The Ghost attempted to put his hand through the steel beam, and was met with its full, physical force. Stunned, barely able to stand on his shaky legs, the Ghost rasped aloud, "What have you done to me?" He knew that Necrosis could hear his thoughts no matter if he spoke them or stayed silent, but he couldn't help but spit the words out.

This time, Necrosis replied, its voice speaking to the Ghost from his own tech:

"You . . . have done this . . . to yourself, creature."

The Ghost attempted to respond, but his jaw muscles tightened, as if having turned to stone under his skin. He stood like a statue, mouth locked open, and gasped out a sound like air escaping from a bottle of soda, but he couldn't form any words. He attempted to grab his other wrist to disable the final energy inhibitor, which would bring the suit up to 100 percent power. He watched his arm move in slow motion and then stop within inches of his other wrist. If he could just switch off the inhibitor, his Ghost-tech would be at full power, and no system—not even Necrosis's—would be able to withstand him. The power surge would doubtlessly set off S.H.I.E.L.D.'s sensors, but at this point,

S.H.I.E.L.D. was the least of the Ghost's worries. Necrosis was in his head, though, and knew his intention.

The Ghost was paralyzed, his hand mere inches from the inhibitor but unable to make the final move to switch it off.

That wasn't the worst of it. Countless times, he had felt his Ghost-tech extracting data from a system he'd hacked into. That feeling of information flooding his brain was euphoric, and utterly unique. Equally unique was the sensation he felt at this moment.

Necrosis was pulling information *from* the Ghost's mind, extracting it like files from a hard drive. If the Ghost didn't find some way to overpower whatever this thing was, he would be left blank, wiped clean . . . empty.

Truly, a ghost.

Tony stood before Necrosis, his finger hovering over his watch. He knew in his gut that if he gave this thing one inkling that he was a threat, it would attack. What would happen when it did attack, Tony didn't know—and he didn't want to find out by becoming its target. It seemed that Necrosis could understand English, or at least translate its own programmed language into English, so Plan A was to talk to it, extract information, and convince it that he was no threat.

Tony *really* didn't want to go to Plan B.

"Necrosis," Tony repeated, his tone light, measured. "That's your name, huh?"

Necrosis towered over him, its visor glowing brighter by the moment. Tony felt his forehead prickle with sweat. From the way that the head followed every move Tony made, it was clear that it was not a drone, nor a suit of armor. There was no third party operating it. No, this was artificial intelligence.

Exactly *how* intelligent it was remained to be seen.

"My name is Tony Stark," he said. "I'm here because . . . well, because of you. I've created a few artificial intelligences myself. I'm sure you know this, but you have been in an idle state. I'm not quite sure what made that happen . . . hell, I'm not even sure how you got *here*. So in a way, we're on the same page, aren't we?"

Necrosis stared, silent.

"I can help you," Tony said. "We can figure out what happened to you. What—what your purpose is, what you were meant to do. Because all AI is created for something, right? You weren't put here to stand like some statue in a lab. No, you're—"

Tony barely had time to throw himself out of the way when Necrosis's burning, green gaze turned into an *actual* burning stream of green energy that obliterated the floor where Tony had been standing.

Tony tapped the screen of his watch as he rolled over on

his shoulder just in time to avoid another blast. Responding to the command on the watch, Tony's briefcase snapped open. The gauntlet flowed out from his watch, just as the rest of the Iron Man suit flew out of the briefcase in its compact form and latched onto Tony's gauntlet, building itself around him automatically. Tony leapt away from blast after blast from Necrosis, each attack burning a hole in the laboratory's floor. He heard the scientists calling out, and he hoped that they had the sense to get out of the laboratory before Necrosis turned its attention toward them.

Finally, Tony's helmet clamped shut over his face with the sharp clang of metal on metal.

Iron Man stood before Necrosis, which had stopped firing at him. It seemed to be looking at Iron Man with curiosity, its visor flashing. Sleek and angular, Iron Man's armor gleamed with the poison-green light from his robotic foe, and then with red light as well, as the laboratory's alarm began to flash. The core of Iron Man's armor glowed with powerful, white repulsor energy—energy that had once kept Tony Stark alive.

Now, he hoped it would do so again.

From inside the armor, Tony's head-up display—an interface that F.R.I.D.A.Y. projected in his line of vision, displaying his vitals, the suit's power, any external or internal damage, and more—examined Necrosis. Heat signals were rocketing all over, and F.R.I.D.A.Y. was doing a 3-D sweep of the robot's form to determine if there was a weak spot. It took a split second for the results to register on the HUD.

Of course there's no weak spot, Tony thought.

As F.R.I.D.A.Y. continued to silently run her scans, Tony held a glowing gauntlet out at Necrosis. He shot a glance to the side, and was relieved to see that the scientists had turned tail. "You're going to want to stop," he said. "Right now. I don't care how much your name sounds like a metal band. I'll bring you down."

"You . . . have done this . . . to yourself, creature," Necrosis said, punctuating the last word with another powerful blast of green energy from its gaze. Tony met the blast in midair with a repulsor beam, which was instantly absorbed by Necrosis's attack. Tony barely had time to rocket out of the way of the incoming blast, which turned the lab table behind him into a steaming hunk of melted metal.

"Fine. Let's take off the gloves," Tony said, holding both hands out at Necrosis.

A devastating blast of blinding power rushed from Tony's gloves, hitting Necrosis directly in its core. The gargantuan robot was shoved backward, and Tony, his confidence bolstered by seeing Necrosis falter, let loose another overwhelming beam of repulsor energy, pushing himself forward as he forced Necrosis back toward one of the sizzling holes in the floor.

Necrosis's legs buckled, and all of Tony's forward movement stopped.

Necrosis took flight, launching itself at Tony and moving through his repulsor beam as it flew. Tony charged upward, launching himself toward the ceiling in order to avoid Necrosis's tackle. He knew that if the robot got a grip on him, it would very likely be able to rip him free of the armor—and that would be a whole new level of problem.

Knowing that he only had a fraction of a second until Necrosis would turn around and fly toward him again, Tony sped back down toward his enemy. He latched onto Necrosis's back, right below its neck. Its arms flailed in an attempt to reach Tony, but they could only just scratch his armor.

Necrosis paused in the wreckage of the S.H.I.E.L.D. laboratory, standing still in what Tony knew had to be damage upward of $10 million.

Necrosis spoke in a voice that sounded like many men speaking at once, their voices breaking through static. Each word had a different tone, tenor, and volume. It made no sense, which scared the hell out of Tony.

"Will you . . . remain there . . . forever?" it asked.

"What's the game here, huh?" Tony asked, clinging to its back. "Who sent you here?"

"You know . . . what comes next," Necrosis said.

It was right. Tony did.

He braced himself as Necrosis launched itself backward, slamming its back—and Tony—into the wall. Tony held on tightly.

"The wall will break before the suit is damaged," F.R.I.D.A.Y. said. "Whatever substance Necrosis's hull is made out of, however, is far more resilient than this Iron Man model."

"Yeah?" Tony groaned as Necrosis slammed backward again. "Let's put that to the test."

"The point, is, sir, you cannot let it pin you against a substance as hard as the armor. Considering its speed and strength, it would take little effort to crush you."

"How about you tell me some good news?" Tony said. "Weaknesses, targets, a way to hack into its system. Something!"

"I'm trying. It's—"

"Try HARDER!" Tony barked as Necrosis slammed him, drywall billowing around them like fog. "We don't—"

"Get away from the robot, Stark!"

Maria Hill's voice somehow rose above the crashing, screeching sounds of Tony's armor scraping against Necrosis as the two of them turned the laboratory wall into dust.

Tony threw himself off of Necrosis, flying between the killer robot and Maria Hill, who stood at the entrance of the laboratory, a gun the size of a moped balanced on her shoulder, its muzzle glowing with a brilliant, red light.

That's a new toy, Tony couldn't help but note, as absurd as the circumstances were. Behind Hill, a crew of almost twenty armored S.H.I.E.L.D. agents flooded onto the balcony, each of them toting M4 carbine assault rifles that they pointed down at Necrosis.

"No!" Tony snapped, keeping an eye on Necrosis, certain that it would attack again at any moment. "No more men down here. This thing is—"

"I have more backup coming, Stark. This is a *rescue* mission. We're getting you *out* of here, now!" Hill shouted. "Step away from the item. We can*not* allow it escape the laboratory. This room is built to withstand extreme force, but the rest of the building—"

"No," Tony said, not budging. "Get out, now, and I'll handle this. You called me here knowing this could happen. Let me do this, Hill. You bring in more men, this thing just has more targets."

"Stand *clear*!" Hill barked. "This is *not* why I called you down here, Tony. We're clearing this bunker and sealing the robot in. Move!"

Necrosis surveyed them, the emerald flames that passed for its eyes in its crystal visor expanding and retracting, matching the rhythm of a heartbeat. Tony knew if it aimed at that group of agents, they wouldn't be able to avoid the blast like he had. He didn't have nearly enough data on Necrosis to form an actual plan, but Tony knew that he had to get these men—and Hill—far away from it before things went further south.

"It's more powerful than you think, Hill! It's cutting through the concrete—you can't seal it in!" Tony snapped back, sweeping his gaze around the room. His head-up display pulled up a 3-D blueprint of the building, showing where the holes that Necrosis had bored in the floor led to. Most of them led toward a concrete bunker, while others seemed to lead to a room of secret files—not an ideal place for what was going to go down. No matter what protections this room had, Tony knew that Hill was wrong—he needed to get this thing out of the building. If he engaged it in full-on combat, even though they were surrounded by concrete and steel, they would bring the whole place down.

"I said out of the way, Tony!" Maria Hill shouted, punctuating her words with a blast from her weapon. The red laser beam shot from the glowing muzzle of her weapon and hit Necrosis in the visor.

Necrosis's head spun around in response with a mechanical whine, but when it clicked back into place, there wasn't so much as a scuff on the visor. Tony felt Maria Hill tense behind him as he prepared for Necrosis's counterattack.

"Do you wish . . . for violence . . . to be your final act?" Necrosis boomed.

"Pacifist, are you?" Hill said. "Security footage suggests otherwise."

"I am . . . no agent of peace," Necrosis replied, the pulse of its eyes quickening. "I am . . . the result . . . of war."

Tony's HUD examined the facility's blueprint, zooming in on the area of the laboratory behind Necrosis and all the way to the left, where row upon row of glass supply cabinets were set up. There was a hatch on the other side of the lab that led down to an emergency escape, most likely in case the elevators malfunctioned. The escape, a concrete tunnel, led under the entire laboratory and then up and out through a back exit in S.H.I.E.L.D.'s facility.

Just like that, Tony had his plan. It wasn't by any means a *good* plan, and perhaps not even achievable. But it was all he had.

"Maybe you don't understand your current situation," Hill said to Necrosis. "You're speaking of war, and yet there's one of you, and—"

"Yeah, go ahead Hill, talk to the bloodthirsty robot like it's a person," Tony said, ready to put his scheme into action. He could tell that Necrosis's curiosity about Maria Hill and her agents was waning. "Get out of here. Now. Trust me."

Without another word, Maria Hill cranked back the gear on her weapon, and a scalding, red laser beam shot out of her gun, four times the size of the first shot. Tony threw himself to the ground just in time to avoid being clipped by the blast.

"Told you to move out of the way," Hill said as the laser

sent Necrosis stumbling back, farther even than Tony's repulsor blasts had. Hill advanced on the robot as Tony flew up into floating position, shaking his head.

"You almost shot me with a gigantic laser," Tony said, barreling toward Necrosis. "Where did you get that thing anyway? It's kind of awesome. Don't hide awesome things from me."

"I knew you'd duck," Hill said, launching another blast at the robot as the rest of the agents spread out in the room, covering other agents who were ushering out the scientists that hadn't already escaped. "Well, I was pretty sure."

Tony matched the impact of the laser with a surge of repulsor energy, pushing Necrosis toward the glass cabinets. Necrosis stumbled again, this time unleashing a vicious stream of green power from its visor. Thrown off its target by Tony and Hill's assault, it faltered, and its energy beam swept across the room and arched up, cutting through the ceiling with a sound that made Tony fear that it would set the entire room ablaze if he didn't direct it out of there, fast.

"Sir, above you!" F.R.I.D.A.Y.'s voice chimed in. Tony looked up just in time to see half of the glass casing that had originally stored the then-idle Necrosis careening down from the ruined ceiling, right toward Maria Hill, who was proceeding toward her target, unaware that she was about to be crushed.

In one fluid motion, Tony swept down toward Hill

and grabbed the twenty-five-foot glass case right before it would've crashed down on her. Holding on to the gigantic case, Tony flew back toward Necrosis, lifting the glass over his head as high as he could without scraping the ceiling.

Tony slammed the thick casing over Necrosis's head. It shattered on impact, sending thick chunks of glass scattering around the room.

"Told you that thing wouldn't hold it!" Tony called out to Hill as Necrosis turned toward the agents on the balcony. A young agent, who Tony thought couldn't have been more than twenty-five, took a shot at the gargantuan robot. The bullet hit Necrosis with a pitiful *clink*.

Necrosis responded with the most powerful stream of energy it had unleashed yet. Tony blasted toward the balcony and threw himself into the agent with more force than he'd intended, launching his own blast of repulsor power to meet Necrosis's deadly force in midair. The agent was crumpled beneath Tony, probably concussed from the impact of the Iron Man armor slamming into him with such force, but that was better than being a pile of ash.

"Hill, get them out of here! Now!" Tony shouted, pushing back against the green energy with his repulsors, giving it everything he had.

"We're expending massive amounts of energy," F.R.I.D.A.Y. warned. "Critical tolerances are being reached, and—"

"Pull from reserves, pull from everything we've got!" Tony shouted. He pushed himself off the balcony and flew toward the flaming green beam as Necrosis bore down over him, leaning in to its deadly blast. Once the agents behind Tony had dragged the young, unconscious agent away and into the elevator from which they'd arrived, Tony pushed off of Necrosis's blast and let it hit the floor.

"Hill, you get out of here, too!" Tony hollered. "Now!"

"Not a chance." Hill aimed at Necrosis, but it easily avoided the blast, not even bothering to turn her way. It was focused on Tony.

Tony ran toward the glass cabinets as Necrosis chased him with the green beam, leaving a fiery path on the floor as it attempted to apprehend Tony. When Tony got to the corner he'd been attempting to work Necrosis into, he whizzed around in a zigzag motion as Necrosis's beam ate away at the floor. Finally, seemingly realizing that Tony was toying with it, Necrosis did exactly what Tony hoped.

It charged at him.

"We in position, F.R.I.D.A.Y.?" Tony asked, floating over the flaming floor.

"In seconds, sir, but the floor is still sturdy enough to support Necrosis's weight," F.R.I.D.A.Y. replied. "It will burn out, but—"

"Not waiting for that," Tony said, his eyes locked on Necrosis as it got closer and closer.

"In place!" F.R.I.D.A.Y. said.

Tony flew down toward Necrosis, holding his hands out, palms facing forward. He let out a great blast of energy, not at the robot, but at its feet. Tony's repulsor power blasted the floor out from under Necrosis and, before it could react, it fell through the ruined concrete and tile toward the tunnel below.

Back in the laboratory, Maria Hill turned toward the balcony as a new squadron of agents emerged, all of them equipped with laser blasters that matched hers. She was stunned by how quickly it had all happened, and was relieved to see that Agent Forester was conscious and standing on his own among them, despite the blood that trickled down his forehead. For a horrible moment, she thought that Necrosis might have gotten him before Tony pushed him away, but there he was, still holding on to his gun and ready to continue their mission.

Maria hurried up the stairs and patted Forester on the shoulder absently as she surveyed the room. A sprinkler system had come alive the moment the flames from the holes Necrosis had bored in the floors began to eat up the walls, but even though the water began to extinguish the flames, the damage was done. The laboratory had been designed to keep any explosion from damaging the foundation of the facility above, and that protection remained in place, but the equipment itself and the flooring was completely destroyed.

"I've never seen so much force from a single source," Hill said. "Stark could barely keep up. We have to cut it off before it exits the building."

Hill motioned for her men to go ahead of her. Speaking into her Bluetooth piece, she rattled off orders.

"We need a fire unit in the south laboratory, now," she said. "I have a squad moving out, and I want teams armed to the teeth blocking every part of the facility that intersects with the southeast hallway. Give me a location on our problem, over."

Agent Judith Klemmer's voice chimed in. "We have a visual, Director Hill. Stark and the item have emerged in the underground tunnel and are both en route to the southeast exit. But—"

"But? What's *but*?" Hill snapped, hurrying out of the lab.

"I believe, Director Hill, that we have *another* problem."

The Ghost could do nothing but watch in mute dread as two armed S.H.I.E.L.D. agents, supported by twin cords that extended up farther than he could see, descended toward him from the top of the elevator shaft. They came to a stop, standing on a platform perpendicular to the beam on which the Ghost stood, immobile.

"We've got him!" bellowed one of the agents, a hulking, bearded man with beady eyes and a neck the size of a normal man's waist. "Identify yourself!"

The Ghost didn't—couldn't—reply. Both of them had their weapons trained on his helmet.

"You heard him," the other agent said. She was thin and short with a scar on the side of her face. A burn mark, it appeared.

The Ghost stood in silence, half hoping they would shoot him where he stood. The instantaneous death would be less frightening than falling down the never-ending shaft. Even more terrifying, Necrosis was still working its way through the Ghost's system, erasing all of the data that made up his memories, his power . . . everything he was. He would rather the immediate comfort of a bullet than that.

As the agents stared him down, waiting for him to respond, the Ghost wished, for the first time since he'd bonded his body and consciousness to his battlesuit, that he could go offline. He'd never mourned his old life. He was too bent on getting revenge on those who had wronged him, and on the corporation that had ruined his life so long ago. When that was done, and the people that had taken everything he cared about away from him were dead and buried, the Ghost had dedicated his life to taking down people like them—people who hurt others in the name of corporate greed. The Ghost had been alone in this mission for a long time. In his world, the buzz of the modern age's omnipotent networks was his only constant.

Now, it was killing him.

"Look at this guy," the scarred agent said, gesturing with her gun. "I think he's messed up. I'm calling it in." She spoke into her comm device, alerting Director Hill that she'd found the intruder.

The brawny agent stretched out a hand in front of the Ghost's helmet, and snapped his fingers. "Hello?" he called, before chuckling. He flicked the helmet with his thick finger and, for a moment, the Ghost thought the battlesuit might topple over and fall the rest of the way down the shaft.

"What do you think it is?" the scarred agent asked, keeping her gun pointed at the helmet as she fastened her comm device back onto her belt. "Maybe one of Stark's spare suits?"

"I don't know. Doesn't look like the Iron Man armor to me." The muscular agent swung on his cord toward the Ghost, landing safely on the beam. He stood still for a minute, his weapon pointed at the Ghost, who longed to deliver a sharp kick to the brute's feet, knocking him down the shaft. The agent grabbed the Ghost's arm roughly, right above the wrist. A glimmer of hope swelled within the paralyzed villain's chest as the agent tugged him forward, his hand right above the power inhibitor.

"Nope," the agent said, releasing the Ghost's arm with a

grimace. "There's someone in here. I feel him through the suit. He feels . . ."

"What?"

"He feels cold."

Maria Hill's voice sounded over the comm device: "Bring him into holding."

"Last chance, then," the scarred agent said from behind the gun. "Either way, you're coming back with us. You've trespassed on government property. Make this easy on yourself and tell us who you are."

The Ghost stood helpless, unable to respond.

"Have it your way," the brawny agent said, bringing his hand down to the Ghost's wrist, right on the power inhibitor. He gave the Ghost a sharp pull toward him, shifting the inhibitor to the off position. "Let's get this freak show processed. I don't know about you, but I want to get down to that robot fight."

The scarred agent opened her mouth to speak, but the Ghost cut her off with a sinister snicker. She and the brawny agent raised their guns as the Ghost drifted over them, his battlesuit glowing as his power rose to full capacity. Electricity crackled from the tubing on the back of his suit, snapping and buzzing, and his snicker built to a horrible, echoing laugh.

"Fire!" the scarred agent called.

The Ghost felt like he was emerging from water as

Necrosis's hold over him slipped away. Floating into the air, he watched the bullets pass through his intangible body, much to the horror of the two guards. He felt Necrosis's pull, still, but it no longer paralyzed him; no longer kept him anchored to his physical being. And after he dealt with the more immediate threat, he'd make sure that Necrosis could never harm him again.

He swooped down toward the agents, bullets continuing to whizz through his incorporeal form. He flew straight into them, taking on physical form at the moment of impact, sending both agents off of the ledge.

"Boo!" the Ghost shouted.

Their ropes caught, stopping them from falling to their deaths—if only for a moment. Gazing down at them from the ledge on which they'd been standing just seconds prior, the Ghost slashed the cords with his needle-sharp claws.

The Ghost floated through the wall, leaving the elevator shaft behind, satisfied by the dwindling screams as the agents fell. His heart raced with growing rage as his battlesuit's system rebooted, refreshing both itself and his memory, and the Ghost floated through wall after wall, moving down and across the building toward Necrosis. The surge of power had allowed the Ghost to reboot entirely, freeing him from Necrosis and giving him control of his own body once again, but could still feel the robot's pulsing signal, stronger than ever.

The Ghost emerged from the wall and into an open hall-way, which flashed with red lights as agents raced through them. The entire building was on alert.

"Good," the Ghost whispered, leering at an agent who caught his gaze as he phased through another wall. "You *should* be scared."

As the Ghost proceeded, he directed the full extent of his power toward Necrosis's system. Before, when Necrosis had just woken and the Ghost's inhibitors were on, the robot's network seemed so immense and alien. Now, the flashing, violent light that had lashed out at the Ghost before seemed smaller, more distant.

This time, the Ghost knew what to look out for and, with his suit operating at full power and Necrosis distracted by Stark, the robot had no hope of maintaining its defense. The Ghost felt his own system extended out from him, push-ing through Necrosis's firewalls, falling over the dwindling flame that was its remaining resistance like a dark shadow swallowing up all light. The Ghost reached out and felt the light move toward him.

"Yesssss," the Ghost hissed. "*There* we are."

The Ghost felt the bond in his bones as his Ghost-tech wormed through Necrosis's system. When he moved his fin-gers, he didn't only clench his own fist—he flexed Necrosis's claw. When he gazed out in front of him, he saw two images, as if his brain had split into a two-screen setup: he saw the

S.H.I.E.L.D. facility through his own battlesuit, and now he saw Iron Man through Necrosis's visor, blasting off ineffectual repulsor rays at the robot as the two of them crashed into an open hallway.

"Hey, Necrosis," the Ghost whispered, and he felt nothing but a distant tremor in response. It had come close, but he now stood victorious. "*You* should be scared, too."

The game was about to change.

Tony had successfully blasted Necrosis into the tunnel, but if he knew Maria Hill, he only had a few moments before the immediate area was once again loaded with S.H.I.E.L.D. agents attempting to "rescue" him. Tony needed to get Necrosis out of the building before anyone else got hurt, and that would entail forcing the robot to chase him all the way up the ramped tunnel and toward the building's exit, which was a huge risk. There was always the chance that Necrosis would turn around and launch an attack at the facility from outside, but Tony knew that no matter how far down they were, Necrosis would burn everything in sight until it had made its way up through the building, including the agents attempting to seal it in.

Tony couldn't think of any other way. He had to get Necrosis away from everyone who was not currently in an Iron Man suit.

Necrosis gained its bearings and stood to its full, twenty-foot height, its head crashing through the concrete ceiling above them as it rocketed toward Tony. Seeing the opportunity, Tony took advantage of Necrosis's momentary sightlessness and took off, moving directly for the exit. He dodged deadly discharges from Necrosis as the deadly robot pulled its head out of the ceiling, now pursuing Tony with ill intent.

Tony watched the oncoming blasts from behind through his HUD, weaving in a loopy pattern to avoid blast after blast as they rocketed toward the security checkpoint at the exit.

"You will be the first to die," Necrosis boomed. "The first to pay . . . for this world's wrongs."

They rounded the final turn of the tunnel, approaching the exit that F.R.I.D.A.Y. showed Tony on the HUD. To Tony's horror, a team of agents was already positioned at the exit, all drawing their guns to meet Necrosis. Tony gestured wildly, speeding up as he came at them.

"Go, go, go!" Tony demanded. "Out of the way!"

With Iron Man barreling toward them, they had no choice but to comply, diving to the side like some kind of synchronized dance move as Tony careened through the weapons detector, which issued a high-pitched siren as he passed. Necrosis was right behind him, and all Tony could do was hope against hope that it would lock its sights on him and ignore the scattering agents.

Tony blasted through the first set of doors leading toward the emergency exit. F.R.I.D.A.Y.'s blueprint told him he had one more set to go through, and a heat analysis confirmed that there were no warm bodies between him and the final doors.

"Here we go," Tony said to himself.

Necrosis was right on his tail, sending out ceaseless shots of green flames. The attacks were far more difficult to avoid at close range, and a few of them grazed Tony's armor, sending flashes of heat through the suit.

Not a good sign, Tony thought.

Finally, Tony saw the last set of steel-reinforced doors at the end of the hall and prepared a blast to take them down. Just as he was about to unleash his mightiest beam of repulsor energy, a wet, icy chill passed through his body. Tony's flight faltered from the pure physical shock of it and he watched in confused horror as Necrosis, suddenly intangible, passed *through* him like a patch of cold fog.

Tony, stunned, shook it off and landed on his feet. He watched as Necrosis, whose hull was now shining with a blue, pallid glow, phased through the doors in front of him and disappeared.

"F.R.I.D.A.Y.!" Tony shouted. "What was that? What's going on?"

"Necrosis's energy patterns have dramatically changed," F.R.I.D.A.Y. chimed in as Tony stared at the place where the robot had been just a second earlier. "It appears that something has remotely shut its system down, replacing its previous mode of operation with entirely new protocols."

Cursing, Tony charged toward doors. He was furious at himself for stopping, but he had been so stunned by Necrosis's latest display of power that he couldn't help himself. "Track it! We can't lose this thing! Do you hear me, F.R.I.D.A.Y.?" Tony yelled as he stuck his iron-clad fingers into the partition between the doors. He forced them open, gritting his teeth as the doors screeched in protest. Tony emerged from S.H.I.E.L.D.'s headquarters and looked up into the sky, which had darkened to a cool blue since he'd joined Maria Hill on her jet back to the facility.

"Sir, Necrosis has—" F.R.I.D.A.Y. said.

"No," Tony snapped, cutting her off. "No, don't tell me that!"

Tony's face mask snapped up, and he squinted at the empty sky. Necrosis was gone.

"Give me something, F.R.I.D.A.Y.," Tony said, scanning the sky above, hoping it would double back and attack. "I need a location, now. We didn't just get this thing out of S.H.I.E.L.D. only to let it loose on the world."

"It's jumping from network to network," F.R.I.D.A.Y.'s voice said, cool and measured. She wasn't programmed to panic, but her calm tone was ramping up Tony's anxiety in a way that made him yearn to hit something. Hard. "Necrosis is beyond—"

"Beyond anything we've seen, yeah, great," Tony snapped. "Stellar. We can't track it. I'm right, yeah? We can't track it."

"Not yet, sir," F.R.I.D.A.Y. said.

"Not yet," Tony repeated, as a unit of agents emerged from the building, joining him on the field. "Not *good*."

Maria Hill stalked toward Tony, backed by a team of agents that jogged out of the facility and spread out over the ground, their weapons pointed skyward.

"I want a quinjet prepped for takeoff immediately," Hill said. "Establish ground teams at every government facility within the hour. We are on high alert until we find this hunk of junk. Do you hear me? Move!"

Tony turned away from her and tried to slow his breathing, but Hill grabbed his shoulder and made him face her. She arms spread in incredulity. "It got away?"

Tony opened his mouth to explain, but then caught himself. He narrowed his eyes, glaring at Maria Hill and trying to calm his growing rage. He knew that if he started talking, he would blame Hill—and maybe she was to blame. But Tony knew that it wasn't Hill who had led Necrosis out of the facility and into the general public without even getting a glimpse at the direction in which it had headed.

No, that was all on him.

"What happened, Stark?" Hill asked.

Toy ignored her question. "You're going to tell me why that thing was in your lab. Now. No excuses, no—no red tape, nothing. We just woke up a twenty-foot deathbot named after gangrene, and that deathbot seems to have no qualms with destroying . . . well, just about everything," Tony said. "Where did it come from?"

Hill stared at Tony, deadpan. "Sure, Tony. Because keeping you apprised of where we found it is *clearly* the highest priority at the moment."

"You want my help taking this down? Let me help you. Tell me everything, Hill. I mean it."

"Fine," Hill said. "I'll send you the entire file. But you know what? Maybe you should be less worried about where it came from and more worried about where it's *going*."

CHAPTER FIVE

I Go Where They Can't

Three men armed with military-grade assault rifles stood in front of a small, wooden building in the middle of the woods. The sign out front read *The Forest Preserve of Tipton County, New Jersey*. Acres of trees stretched for miles around all sides of the little structure, tucking it safely away from civilization.

One of the men had a heavily chewed toothpick sticking out of his mouth. Another was noisily chowing down on an enormous sub with thick slabs of deli meat stacked on it. The other man was staring at the screen of his cell phone through squinted eyes, a permanent scowl etched on his creased face.

"*Madon*," the scowling man said, shaking his head. "This freakin' thing. Can't get a signal for nothing out here."

"Not supposed to be on your phone, Albie," the man with the toothpick said. "Boss catches you on your phone, he's gonna make a thing of it."

"Bah," the scowling man—Albie—said, shoving the

phone back into his pocket. "I was just trying to get on my e-mail. My nephew told me he sent pictures of his new kid to me. I don't know why he can't show me an actual picture in person, like a real human. These freakin' phones."

"I don't get a signal out here, either," the man with the sandwich said, swallowing loudly. "Tried texting the wife earlier and it never sent. I think I heard one of those white coats in the lower level say they're blocking the signal."

"Blocking the signal," the man with the toothpick repeated, shaking his head incredulously. "We're in the middle of nowhere, you moron. There's just no service, Sal."

"Hey, *I* didn't say it," the man with the sandwich—Sal—said. "I told you, I just heard one of those white coats talking. He said they're doing this GPS thing, right? Where, if someone tries to come to the forest, right, their signal gets scrambled, points them away from us. That way, no one finds us here by mistake."

"Basement dwellers," the man with the toothpick said, spitting. "It's not fair, all of them sitting in the AC down there while we're standing around like idiots."

"Maybe *you're* standing around like an idiot, Rusty," Sal said. "I'm just standing around."

"I'm bored out of my mind!" Rusty, the man with the toothpick, said. "We've been doing this nine hours a day, five days a week. It's torture."

"Maybe," Sal said. "But it's worth the money."

"You know what . . . I've been wondering," Albie said. "With a guy like the boss in *there*, what do you think they need us out here for?"

"What do you mean?" Rusty asked.

"Come on," Albie said, jerking his head back toward the building. "Way I hear it, the boss can shoot lighting from his hand, he can fly, he's got super strength—"

"Oh!" Rusty cried, and threw up his arms in annoyance. "We don't talk about that, do you hear me? Didn't Nefaria's men say the same thing to you as they did to me? Were you not in that same room, sitting next to me, accepting the same deal?"

"Hey, I'm just saying," Albie said, stepping away in a gesture of mock defeat. "Makes you wonder, is all, why he's got guys like us out here when he's—"

"It doesn't make me wonder," Sal chimed in. "We're not getting paid to wonder what sort of super-human crap the boss can do. We stand guard, we ask no questions, we deposit the cash."

Ignoring him again, Albie shook his head. "I'm just saying, is all. Makes you wonder."

"What did I just say?" Sal snapped. "You don't know who's listening to this conversation, Albie. Clearly, these are very paranoid people. Which makes me *not* want to get caught 'wondering.' So shut your face before—"

He was cut off by a squealing whistle that sounded like

a bottle rocket. They looked up, afraid that they were about to be attacked—but when the glowing green thing appeared in the sky, they didn't have the chance to ponder if it was a monster, a UFO, a crashing plane, or a drone before it rocketed down to the ground and landed with a deafening boom, sending a shower of dirt over them.

The three men looked up at Necrosis, gaping at it in silent astonishment. For a moment, they stood there, unsure if the best thing to do was to run, call for Nefaria, or shoot at it—whatever *it* was.

Rusty made the decision, and the other two followed suit: he lifted his gun, pointed it at Necrosis's head, and pulled the trigger.

The other two men followed suit. They kept firing, letting off rounds of shots that would've brought almost any other intruder down, until they ran out of ammunition. Albie fumbled to reload. Sal grabbed his arm with a shaky hand.

"L-l-look," said Sal, whose sandwich had fallen on the grass. He pointed up at Necrosis, his finger trembling. There wasn't even a scuff mark on its hull.

"Call for backup," Rusty snapped, holding his rifle steady even though he knew full well that it wouldn't protect him. "One of you idiots, call for backup now!"

"That's not necessary."

The warbling, echo of a voice came not from the towering robot's head, but from its core. All three men jumped backward in shock as the Ghost, shimmering in his battle-suit, floated out from the inside of Necrosis.

The three men raised their guns at once, all of them pointing at the Ghost's helmet.

"Henh," the Ghost chuckled, standing in front of Necrosis, still intangible. They could see the sea of trees through his translucent body, stretching on for miles. "Go ahead, if you really want to. Shoot me."

"Who are you?" Albie asked.

"Did you hear what I said?" Rusty yelled. "I told you to call for backup, now! We have a situation!"

As Rusty grabbed his comm device with his spare hand, while still holding the rifle out at arm's length, the Ghost stepped forward, bowing slightly. "Apologies for the confusion, gentlemen. Count Nefaria is expecting me and my . . . friend here. Tell him that the Ghost has arrived with his present."

The three man shared a look, dumbfounded.

"Hey," the Ghost said, his voice thick with wicked delight. He gestured to the ground. "You dropped your sandwich."

Once he was given clearance to enter the compound, the Ghost phased back inside of Necrosis. The exterior of Nefaria's stronghold was no more than a log cabin—believable for the office of a forest preserve, to be sure, but the small structure didn't betray the truth of the gigantic, multilayered complex underground. To get Necrosis inside, though, he had to make the robot incorporeal and phase through the safe house until they reached the laboratory.

Now that the Ghost had trumped Necrosis's defenses completely, he had begun to feel more at one with its hulking form. Even when he'd managed to use his Ghost-tech to make Necrosis incorporeal to facilitate their escape from Iron Man and S.H.I.E.L.D., its system still felt alien to him. Like trying to write with his left hand. Necrosis's AI was stifled by the Ghost-tech—made dormant once again—allowing the Ghost to essentially *drive* the robot, using its powers and weapons with his own network. But still, it was big, unwieldy, and far more intricate than the Ghost's own battlesuit, so there had been something of a learning curve. Now, though, in Nefaria's facility, the Ghost moved the robot with confidence and grace.

The Ghost phased Necrosis into the ground level of the safe house—the wooden cabin—which was, the Ghost supposed, Nefaria's version of a security check. There, visitors were greeted by a room full of men in leather jackets who shot you if you didn't have an appointment. They'd been alerted to Necrosis's arrival, of course, but every one of them flinched as the incorporeal robot phased through the wall and disappeared into the ground. The Ghost snickered from within, the sound echoing through Necrosis's body.

The Ghost moved down to the second level. Underneath

the tiny Tipton Forest Preserve facility was a fully operational nightclub for Nefaria and his men (his higher-ranking men who weren't tasked with guarding the entrance or the first level, that is). The floor was complete with dancers and a DJ; all of the staff were members of or related *to* members of Nefaria's inner circle. The Ghost got yet another laugh out of how the entire club came to a halt once Necrosis passed through the ceiling and then sank down through the floor. One oblivious dancer kept writhing on her platform, and the Ghost thought about coming up behind her and saying "boo," but he decided against it. Nefaria's men didn't seem like the most jovial bunch, even when they were drinking and dancing.

The Ghost moved farther underground, to the third level, which was boring by comparison: a winding hallway with doors that the Ghost could only assume led to offices and bedrooms. He knew that this was where he'd first spoken with Nefaria, but he'd been led into the facility with a bag over his helmet that blocked his vision. He'd also felt a rather strong power dampener blocking the networks within the facility. Nefaria's people might not have been on the Ghost's level, but they'd worked hard to keep this place a secret.

Finally, he phased one floor below that to the final level— Nefaria's think tank, which contained the only people in the entire building who didn't balk at Necrosis's entrance. No, these people seemed transfixed. The think tank was unlike any the Ghost had ever seen, closer in lighting and mood to the nightclub on level two than to S.H.I.E.L.D.'s sterile laboratory where Necrosis had been stored. It was gigantic, with multiple projects being worked on at once—mostly weapons. There wasn't a soul in the entire lab that looked a day over twenty-five, except for Count Nefaria himself, who sat in a cushy armchair off to the side. There was a second, empty chair next to him.

Nefaria patted the seat. "Come. Leave the machinery for my friends here. You and I have much to discuss."

Nefaria sipped espresso from a tiny cup, his slender legs crossed as he watched the men and women hard at work attempting to dismantle Necrosis, which the Ghost had phased out of to talk business with Nefaria.

"Nice place, by the way," the Ghost said to Nefaria, who had fallen silent after the Ghost explained how he'd hacked Necrosis, and what exactly he knew about the robot . . . which, despite their merging of networks, still wasn't much. That information was buried deep. "It would almost be inconspicuous if you didn't have three guys who look like something out of *The Godfather* out there with AR-15s pointed at every raccoon that rustles some leaves."

"Ah," Nefaria said, smiling knowingly. "You can never be

too careful. I've been on high alert since you and I came to our agreement. When dealing with S.H.I.E.L.D., you must be prepared for whatever tricks they will pull."

"No need to worry about that," the Ghost said. "They couldn't trace me if they had a hundred years to catch up to my tech. They're busy searching the skies, but I do most of my traveling underground. As soon as Necrosis and I were clear of the facility and out of sight, we phased through pavement."

"Bravo," Nefaria said, lifting his cup.

"That's why you pay me the big bucks, isn't it?" the Ghost said. "I go where they can't."

"Indeed," Nefaria said. He slid a briefcase across the table. "Speaking of which . . . I won't be insulted if you count it."

"I can tell what kind of man you are. You'd sooner shoot me than short me," the Ghost said. He watched a muscular woman in protective gear trying to cut through Necrosis's hull with an oxyacetylene torch. Her skin was glistening with sweat, suggesting that she had been trying to do so for a long while, and she'd only managed to make a cut six inches long. At that rate, the Ghost surmised, it would take all day and night to complete the first step of the plan.

But it was working. The Ghost knew from his bond with Necrosis that it would, but it was fascinating watching it happen. Tony Stark had blasted Necrosis with all he had, and here these kids were chipping away at it, bit by bit, patiently weakening its hull with their flames. That's all it took. Patience.

"Explain to me again," Nefaria said, "exactly how you know what you know. You'd said that the robot's system overpowered yours at first. How can we guarantee that this Necrosis won't trump your control once again? And, once it has been broken down into parts, how can we ensure that it won't . . . misbehave?"

"Once I'm in, I'm in," the Ghost said. "It's system is foreign, and more powerful than you could imagine, but if you're able to adopt its technology, it shouldn't have any adverse effect on any of your other systems. I assaulted its systems with my own at only fifty-percent power. I was trying not to pop up on S.H.I.E.L.D.'s security, but it was an error in judgment. This thing's power is out of this world. Literally."

Nefaria sneered in response to the pun. "And it came out of its conflict with Stark completely undamaged?"

"You bet. That thing right there is completely Iron Man–proof."

"Heat," Nefaria said, watching in fascination as the woman continued to apply the torch to Necrosis's core. "If something as simple as a flame could cut through Necrosis, how could Tony Stark not know?"

"It's not heat that can breach the hull," the Ghost said. "It is *prolonged* heat. Whatever Necrosis is made out of is stronger than anything we've got on Earth. Bursts of heat bounce off of it, so nothing short of—what, throwing it in a *volcano* could really extensively damage the material. It's like Silly Putty."

Nefaria sneered. "Silly . . . Putty?"

"If you flick Silly Putty with your finger, it'll just bounce your finger back. But slowly, slowly push your finger into it, and you'll push right through it. Basically, Iron Man can hit Necrosis with whatever he's got, but he's not going to have the time or energy to hit it with enough heat for a long enough time to make a difference. I mean, you know where they dug this thing out of. That's the type of heat we're talking about."

Nefaria nodded, but he was staring at Necrosis with an expression that the Ghost read as disdain. The Ghost, unnerved by Nefaria's demeanor, clapped his hands to his side and stood. "Well. We good?"

Nefaria turned to the Ghost while taking a sip of his espresso. "All of the robot's protocols have been shut down, yes?" he asked, completely ignoring the Ghost's question. "You can confirm, without a shadow of a doubt, that Necrosis will not act . . . unpredictably."

"Necrosis won't act at all," the Ghost said. "I've given you a completely blank slate—shut the whole thing down. Your think tankers should be able to make it do whatever they want."

"What did it want?" Nefaria asked. "Before you gave Necrosis the blank-slate treatment, you were in its network. You surely knew its protocols, its—its reason for existing, no? Why it was created?"

"There was no information on who created it. But, with respect, Mr. Nefaria, take a look at it," the Ghost said. Even lying there idly, it exuded menace. "Why do you *think* it was created?"

Nefaria chuckled, but the Ghost didn't meet his eyes. Instead, he clapped his hands on his sides. "Listen, no offense, but this is normally the time when my benefactor decides to shoot me and take his money back. If it's all the same, I'll be on my way. "

"I respect your honesty," Nefaria said. "In turn, I ask that you respect me enough to hear me out."

The Ghost set the briefcase back on the small, circular table between them and settled into his seat. "I'm listening."

"You may have deduced that I plan to break Necrosis down into weapons . . . hopefully weapons that my people can replicate," Nefaria said. "And—if we can replicate the material it's made from—perhaps even shields, body armor. Maybe, eventually, our own suits to mimic that ridiculous contraption Tony Stark wears. Beyond that, once we are able to analyze its internal system, I hope to replicate its technology as well. But that's long game. More immediately comes our business."

"Right," the Ghost said. "You'd mentioned that you might want me to run another errand for you."

"Understand, Ghost, that I don't offer partnership in this venture lightly. You know that I am a man of pride, and that this pride extends to my family first and foremost. Everything I do, I do for the benefit of them. Those who work with me, side by side, making this family—this home—what it is. They are soldiers."

"Okay?" the Ghost said, wondering if that extended to the three fools outside.

"I say this so that you understand my offer, and what it means to me," Nefaria said. "I had hoped you would stay on board. I will offer you partnership, protection, and more money than you will ever find anything to do with. This in exchange for helping me achieve a goal that will be mutually beneficial in and of itself."

The Ghost stared at Nefaria for a long moment. He'd known this time would come. He'd practiced his answer in his head, envisioning Nefaria's reaction each time. "No."

Watching Nefaria's face fall in person was better than the Ghost had imagined. He almost burst out laughing, but, for his plan to work, he had to keep his cool. He waited for Nefaria to speak.

"Hm," Nefaria continued after a period of silence. "You seem surprised that I'd even ask."

"No. It surprises me that you think I'd *want* to. That I'd

think it's some kind of honor," the Ghost said. "Remember, the alternative is me going to Cancún."

Nefaria let out a barking laugh. "Yes. A city of sun for the dead man confined to his suit. If you left here, you'd ask my private jet to fly you to your home. Let's drop the pretense and talk to each other honestly, as men. I chose you to obtain this weapon because I knew that if everything I'd heard about you was true, that you could do it. And here we are, with a robot that could initiate doomsday itself under our control. I was right. Right about you, right about what Necrosis can be for us."

"You want me to stick around because . . . what?"

"Because this," Nefaria said, gesturing to Necrosis and the woman cutting through his hull. "*This* is the work of a snail. As brilliant as these young men and women may be, how long will it take us to get in? To understand the technology, to repurpose it, to weaponize it? This is slow, directionless . . . whereas you, Ghost, you brought me my biggest win in a very long time in two days. Like you said, you go where others can't. If you work with my people, with *me*, we can do spectacular things. That makes you a man I want by my side. Not a man I want to simply make a delivery."

"That's not what I did. I gave you a deadly weapon that will very likely lead to *more* deadly weapons for you."

"And what are you, then?" Nefaria said. "Are you yourself not a weapon? An angry, potent weapon that is eager to fire itself at our many shared enemies. You told me that Tony Stark being alive doesn't make you lose sleep at night. But I know your history. I know what unfeeling corporations and men like Stark have done to you. What if I told you that I want you to help me create an answer to any problem that we may ever have again? What if I told you I believe you can use Necrosis to weaponize not *me*, but us . . . and that I would stand by you and burn down everything that stands in our way . . . not because I can't do it myself, but because I believe that you will? Under your guidance, my team can disassemble Necrosis and build an arsenal. Use it against *whomever* you want to obliterate, and I will stand by your side. Full support."

Nefaria looked into the curved glass of the Ghost's helmet, but even though the Ghost's eyes were unseen, both men could feel that their gazes were locked. The only sound in the room was the persistent hum of the torch.

"You know what?" the Ghost said. He tried to hide the note of triumph in his voice. He knew that he'd succeeded at allowing Nefaria to believe that he'd convinced the Ghost to go along with his plan. Meanwhile, the Ghost's own plans were just beginning to fall into place. Leaning back in the cushy armchair, the Ghost folded his hands behind his helmet. "I'll take that espresso now."

CHAPTER SIX

Shiny Happy Robot

Lieutenant Colonel James "Rhodey" Rhodes was jarred awake by what sounded to him like a cymbal crash in his basement. He sat up on the couch and, for a moment, thought the sound had come from the television. He'd fallen asleep watching a movie the night before, and now a noisy cartoon was playing. Then, the crash came again. Definitely not the cartoon. Definitely in the basement.

Narrowing his eyes, he stood and padded toward the basement, grabbing the baseball bat that was leaning against the wall below his shelves of sports trophies. It had been a long time since he had been attacked at home, but in his line of work—both the bill-paying kind and the . . . extracurricular kind—one tended to amass a few enemies.

Rhodey was an Avenger: War Machine.

He'd started running with the Avengers due to his friendship with Tony Stark, who seemed to have a singular talent for getting Rhodey into trouble—both the super-heroic kind and the classic kind. Rhodey had even donned the Iron Man suit for a while when Tony ran into some trouble of his own, but became War Machine when Tony picked up his old mantle.

War Machine didn't quite have the rogues' gallery that the other Avengers boasted—he had yet to become mortal enemies with Asgardian volcano monsters or genetically modified World War II criminals—but there was no shortage of moustache-twirling fiends that would love to see Rhodey given a funeral with full military honors. Now, he wondered if one of those moustache twirlers happened to be sneaking around in his basement, where he kept his armor.

Given his current mood, he was beginning to wish someone *would* try to cross him in his home. On a weekend, no less. Some of these super villains just flat out lacked decency. He'd like to show them just how serious War Machine takes a weekend off.

Rhodey slipped out of his shoes so as to not make noise as he crossed onto the creaky kitchen floor, padding slowly toward the door that led down to the basement. It was ajar. Rhodey wasn't sure if it was he who'd left it open; he'd been down there the evening before to grab a bottle of coconut water.

He eased the door open with his foot soundlessly, and moved onto the first step. From his vantage point, he couldn't see anyone, but he heard the faint clinking of metal on metal. He gritted his teeth and tightened his grip on the bat. There was definitely someone down there.

Rhodey descended the stairs as quietly as he could, until he reached the final step. Ready to swing at the first sign of movement, he spun around to face the intruder.

"You picked the wrong house, friend!" he barked, holding the bat in preparation to crack it across the intruder's head. The trespasser—male, tall, wearing a dirty undershirt—had a wrench in his hand and seemed to be in the process of dismantling the War Machine armor that was standing idle in the middle of the basement, its silver surface reflecting the dim light that hung above Rhodey's basement workstation.

Tony Stark turned around to face Rhodey, arching an eyebrow.

"I'm sorry, did you really just say, '*You picked the wrong house, friend*'? Are we in a spaghetti western? Are you the action hero of a direct-to-DVD *Die Hard* sequel?" Tony said, tossing the wrench from hand to hand.

Rhodey lowered the bat. "You're insane."

Tony winked, pointing the wrench at him. "Actually not the first time I got that today. Well, she called me 'crazy.' 'Certifiable.' Basically the same." He turned around and began tinkering with the War Machine armor once again.

Rhodey circled around to face Tony and set the bat next to a gallon of laundry fluid on his washing machine. "You know I have a doorbell, right?"

"Yeah," Tony said, absentmindedly, twirling his moustache as he looked at the armor, as if trying to figure out the answer to an unspoken question. "Yeah, I figured. Maybe an old-fashioned knocker. I don't think this place has been renovated since the '70s. Nice place. Came through the back. Figured I'd let you sleep in while I looked the old suit over. You were snoring. It was adorable." He gestured in the general direction of the stairs that led up to Rhodey's backyard. "Figured you kept the armor down here. I was right. Yay me."

"Tony, you do realize that I programmed that armor to obliterate anyone without my fingerprints who comes within a yard of it while I'm not inside of it. You could've—"

"Nope," Tony said. He shook his wrist, flashing his gleaming watch at Rhodey. "Couldn't have. F.R.I.D.A.Y.'s keen to your security system. Should I lie to you about how long it took me to shut it down? It took me five minutes. That long enough? Five minutes. Very good system, Rhodey."

Rhodey moved his toolbox to the floor so he could sit on his workbench. "Be real with me, man. What's got you making a house call at seven in the morning on a Friday? Isn't this usually around the time when you get to bed?"

"Haven't slept," Tony said. "I . . . let's see, I started the day—yesterday, I guess—by stopping a casino robbery. The Melter."

"The Melter?" Rhodey asked, chuckling. "A Melter incident called for an Iron Man appearance?"

"Gotta have my fun," Tony said, breezily. He rotated

one of the rocket launchers built into the back of the War Machine armor, frowning deeply. "Poor positioning. I owe you an apology. I could do better than this in my sleep. I must have been mad at you. Gonna have to fix this before we head out."

"We're heading out?"

Tony tossed the wrench aside. "First things first. Sent the Melter off to annoy whatever poor unfortunate soul they stick in his cell at county. Went to San Diego, saw a few dogs. Took off for the Bahamas for an all-inclusive weekend with Pepper. Rented the place out. Whole place. It was going to be just us."

"You rented out the whole place," Rhodey repeated. "Who does that?"

"Painfully handsome billionaires, mostly. But then, Maria Hill of all people showed up," Tony continued. "Not someone you want to see at a Bahamian resort. So she came bearing, you know, exactly what you'd expect: bad news. I had to leave Pepper to head *back* to S.H.I.E.L.D. with Hill, where they'd unearthed this . . . this killer robot. *Necrosis*, it called itself."

"A killer robot that *talks*," Rhodey said.

"Talks, shoots green fire, flies, phases through walls," Tony said, shaking his head. "Whole package. It was idle when they found it. They dug it up out of—actually, Hill hasn't told me yet . . . but they unearthed this thing from wherever it was, because *of course they did.* That's what they do. They see something shiny, *'Ooooh, what's this? Looks dangerous. Let's see what makes it tick.'* And now I'm left to clean up the mess."

Rhodey stood, looking Tony in the eye. "That's all I need to hear. I'm in."

An appreciative smile flittered across Tony's lips, but the darkness in his eyes didn't fade. "I couldn't even scratch the damn thing, Rhodey. Now, it's out in the world, God knows where, and I don't know if I can bring it down. F.R.I.D.A.Y. couldn't get a read on its energy source, on what it's made out of, nothing. Nothing. *I* don't know what it's *made* out of."

"So then we find it ourselves. The two of us," Rhodey said. "What's the plan?"

"We're heading to my place. We'll call the Avengers, assemble the whole team. Find Necrosis, launch a full assault. But . . ." Tony turned away from Rhodey and looked the War Machine suit up and down again. "We have to make a few modifications here. Oh, and uh . . . when we get to my place, you go straight to the workshop, okay? I have a feeling I'm going to have a conversation when I get there, and I'd rather you not be around. The past twenty-four hours have been a nightmare even without you hearing Pepper chewing me out."

"Oh, I'd love to hear that. There aren't many things more

entertaining than watching you try to talk your way out of lady trouble," Rhodey said, beaming at him. "Sweet, sweet nectar."

Tony rolled his eyes, clapped Rhodey on the back, and made his way up the back stairs. "Keep being smart and I'm going to turn those rocket launchers into water guns. See you soon."

When Tony arrived home at the spectacular Stark Tower, a sleek and imposing skyscraper that towered over its neighboring buildings in the New York City skyline, he was surprised to discover that he was wrong about Pepper. She wasn't in any of the offices or bedrooms, nor the lounge, where he'd expected to find her sitting with her legs crossed and her face set in that blank stare that she saved for times when Tony *really* messed up.

Tony felt a momentary sinking in his gut. He hoped that she still cared enough to be furious. He needed that—that reminder that he had a life beyond his work, beyond his duty, beyond his obsessions—even if he didn't give that life the attention it deserved. He sighed sharply and walked into the elevator, its doors opening upon his approach, and forced himself to let it go, at least for now.

"Take me to church, F.R.I.D.A.Y.," Tony said, pulling out his cell phone.

"Down we go," F.R.I.D.A.Y. replied, her voice emanating from around the elevator, which began its descent to the workshop.

For now, Tony chose to imagine that Pepper had stayed at the resort and was currently reading a book on the beach, enjoying her peaceful escape. Until he located Necrosis and put it back in the ground where it belonged, that would have to do.

Tony stepped into his sprawling workshop, tapping out a text message to Clint Barton—Hawkeye, a fellow Avenger— as he walked. Compared to Rhodey's workshop, this place looked like he'd stepped into the future. Another section of the workshop lit up with every step he took until he was directly in the center of the room, and computer screens followed him from extendable arms, offering him updates on the projects he'd set in motion while gone. The heat-resistant suit inspired by his run-in with the Melter was 15 percent complete; Next Step for Dogs was at 40 percent, but that meant the preliminary work was finished and he would need to physically be there to put the next stage of work into production.

"Ahem."

That was decidedly not how his good friend Rhodey sounded when he cleared his throat. Tony's eyes shot up and there, standing before the armory where the latest incarnations of the Iron Man suits stood in a dazzling display, was Pepper Potts.

It was the first time Tony ever felt relief upon seeing that you're-in-big-trouble blank stare.

The relief lasted only a moment, though. Tony furrowed his brow and cocked his head to the side as Pepper stared at him. "You're in the workshop. You never come into the workshop alone." He spun around, gesturing toward his glowing, sixteen-screen computer setup, each of which displayed a piece of F.R.I.D.A.Y.'s pink, holographic face. "F.R.I.D.A.Y., you're supposed to let me know who's here *when* they're here."

"Ms. Potts has override powers. Too bad," F.R.I.D.A.Y. said, offering a bright smile.

"Too bad!?" Tony repeated, holding up his hands in mock exasperation, hoping to get a laugh out of Pepper. No such luck.

"You're back sooner than I expected," Pepper said, turning away from him and toward the armory. She put her hand on the glass and looked at the Iron Man suits, which stared back coldly. "I was . . . I just wanted to be in your space. See what new projects you were working on before Hill got to you. See what's keeping you up at night these days."

"I've been at S.H.I.E.L.D. pretty much since I—er, since I left," Tony said, absentmindedly running his fingers along the cool glass as he walked. "And as for what I'm working on, you know, nothing much. Nothing *too* new, anyway. I did start thinking of something on the way to the resort before. Next Step for Dogs. It'll be the biggest thing on the, uh, the injured-house-pet market."

"You already told me about that."

"Right," Tony said. "Right."

Pepper looked up at Tony. Blank stare.

"So, I'm thinking you hate me," Tony said. "Which, I get. We had our thing, I could've stayed—"

"Oh, don't you patronize me," she said, sneering at him. "That's so disappointing, Tony. I told you to go. You think, after all this time, that I don't understand how your mind works?"

Tony scrunched his face, surprised at the direction of this conversation. "Uh . . . no? *No* is the right answer here, gonna go with?"

"I'm fine, Tony," Pepper said. "I'm not upset with you for leaving."

"Good!" Tony said, grinning. "Good, because—"

"I'm upset with you because I don't know if you really wanted to be there to begin with," she said.

"Whoa. Whoa, whoa. That's not even—I wanted to be there. We were having fun. With the beach and the massage, violent as it was, and the—"

"You get in these phases where you're obsessing, where you're searching for some new—some new *muse*," Pepper said. "It's cyclical. If you're not breaking new ground on Iron Man, you're out there looking for something, unable to rest, unable to let your brain slow down for one second until you find a problem that needs fixing—something to throw yourself into so you don't have to just . . . be. Because you can't."

Tony opened his mouth to respond, and then, for once, seeing Pepper's eyes flash with anger, thought better of it.

"That's exactly why I told you to go," Pepper said. "You wanted a project. Something impossible to crack, just so you can *do* the impossible. And here I am again, just left hoping that you'll give yourself a break. Which you never do."

"Is this an incredibly angry way of telling me that you care about me?" Tony said. He felt his phone buzz and glanced down at it. Clint had responded to the text.

Sorry. In Budapest. Big mess here. Stuck for another 48 hours.

Tony cursed silently and shoved the phone back into his pocket.

Pepper shook her head. "You know I care about you," she said. "It just drives me crazy when I look at you, and you're standing in front of me but I can tell you're a million miles away."

Tony and Pepper stood across from each other in loaded silence.

"There's a psycho alien robot on the loose that's named after rotting skin," Tony said lightly.

"I know," Pepper said. "Rhodey told me."

"Rhodey told—" Tony spun around to see Rhodey sitting off to the far side of the shop, leaning against the wall in his War Machine armor, the faceplate pulled back to reveal a simpering grin.

"Sweet, sweet nectar," Rhodey said.

"F.R.I.D.A.Y.!" Tony shouted. "You're really making me consider starting from scratch on your programming."

"Again, sir, Ms. Potts has override powers. Nothing I could do. Might I say, you took that adult conversation uncharacteristically well."

Tony turned toward Pepper incredulously. "You see what I put up with?"

Pepper grabbed Tony's hand, her eyes softening. "When this is over, promise me you'll let yourself breathe. I don't even need to be with you when you do it. I know how you are when you're about to crash, and I don't want to see that happen. Not again."

"I'm good," Tony said, forcing a smile. "I'll breathe. There will be breathing. I promise."

Pepper held his hand for a moment and then sighed heavily before leaving Tony and Rhodey in the workshop.

"Tony, I'm not 'bailing' on you," Captain America said, out of breath. "I'm in Madripoor trying to prevent a hostile takeover of—"

Tony winced and held the cell phone away from his ear until he heard the voice on the other end fall to silence.

"We need the Avengers for this one, Steve. Full roster. I barely dented this thing on my own. I texted Hawkeye and he's off on some vacation in Budapest, and Thor's phone is going straight to voice mail, which I'm gonna guess means he's on a quest to find the One Ring in Asgard or something. I'm coming up short here. I need you to work your magic. Rhodey and I can't handle this one alone."

"Thank you for the vote of confidence!" Rhodey called from behind him.

"I hear you," Cap replied. "Listen, when we're done here, we're going to be on the first plane back. People's lives are at risk here, too, and Falcon and I—"

"You've got Falcon over there?" Tony shouted. "Cap, I don't have time here. For all we know, Necrosis is digging its way to the chewy center of the Earth right now."

"You know I can't leave these people hanging, Tony," Cap said. "I have to run. Keep me updated on Necrosis, and I'll be there as soon as I can. And tell Rhodey I say hi."

"Hey, Cap. You're on speaker," Rhodey said.

"Very cute. Adorable. You know what Necrosis means, right, Cap? It's when skin rots while the person is still alive. Does that sound like a shiny, happy robot to you?"

"I'll be there, Tony."

The call ended, and it took every ounce of self-control

Tony had not to fling his phone across the room. Rhodey walked over to him, shaking his head. "No go from Banner. He's out on S.H.I.E.L.D. business. He texted and said he's going to—"

"Get here as soon as he can, right. At this rate, we're going to have to give Puck and Doctor Druid a call, see what they're up to," Tony said. Over Rhodey's shoulder, he watched as F.R.I.D.A.Y.'s mechanical claws—metallic devices that descended from the ceiling, acting as welding units or water-jet cutters with the grace and precision of a brain surgeon—ran Tony's preprogrammed modifications on Rhodey's War Machine armor. When F.R.I.D.A.Y. was done, the suit would be a great deal lighter and would pack an even bigger wallop.

"F.R.I.D.A.Y.," Tony called out, pointing toward his multiscreen setup on the other side of the room. They lit up pink with F.R.I.D.A.Y.'s face upon Tony's command. "Give me a progress report on our friends in the air."

"You programmed her to be gorgeous," Rhodey noted.

"She's AI," Tony said. "You're sick."

"You programmed her to look that way," Rhodey countered. "*You're* sick."

Tony turned away from Rhodey and checked to see if he'd gotten a text back from Natasha yet. Nothing. "Ignore him, F.R.I.D.A.Y.," Tony said. "Talk to me."

"Five drone-piloted Iron Man suits have been sent out

to track down Necrosis," F.R.I.D.A.Y. replied. "No sightings. The search continues."

Tony nodded, feeling his frustration balloon. He pushed his phone off to the side and spoke aloud: "*Call* Natasha Romanova and put her on speakerphone. She's not answering my texts, so let's go ahead and just call and call and call until she answers." He then looked to Rhodey. "Call Spider-Man. Ten to one he's swinging around a building a few blocks away."

Rhodey nodded as Tony's phone dialed Black Widow. Again. Again.

"Come on, Tony. I can't talk," Natasha Romanova, the Black Widow, answered after the fourth call.

"Hi," Tony said, his voice dripping with saccharine sweetness. "I realize that everyone is incredibly busy, but I have a sentient weapon of mass destruction flying around who-knows-where, and the only Avenger who has time to help me ensure that the world doesn't . . . you know, get destroyed is my good pal Rhodey. I'll have a jet sent your way in ten minutes. Or an Iron Man suit. Or—"

"I appreciate that you're probably dealing with something horrific, but I'm currently staring at a device that will, if I don't diffuse it in the next two minutes and thirty seconds, turn the city of Paris into a black hole," Natasha said. "And then, there are four more just like it planted all throughout the continent of Europe. Wanna trade?"

Tony winced. "I do like Europe."

"Then let me make sure there is a Europe for you to keep enjoying. I'll be there as soon as I can," Natasha said. "And know that I only answered the phone because a personal call from Tony Stark *only* means it's the end of the world."

She ended the call.

Tony looked toward Rhodey, who was finishing up his conversation. "Black hole bomb," Tony said. "That's . . . actually a great excuse. I'm going to use that one the next time I don't want to do something. Way better than Clint's excuse. Budapest. What could've happened in Budapest?"

"Spidey's no good either," Rhodey said. "You know, if we can somehow hold this thing off for two days, we'll have the full support of the team."

"Well, Necrosis didn't say much, but I can confidently say that it didn't seem like an exceptionally *patient* murderous deathbot."

"What did it say, then?" Rhodey asked.

"It said . . . well, first, first it spoke in a language that doesn't exist. Or one that I don't know of, which is unlikely, obviously," Tony said. "Then, it said, 'Hello,' and asked me what my name was. That was in a different voice. After that, it switched back to the original voice, and it was speaking English this time. Said 'I am Necrosis,' and . . ." Tony's lips parted and he stared off into space, cowed into silence by a sudden thought. Finally, he muttered the only word he could think of: "Huh."

Rhodey said, "And?"

"It . . . was having a conversation," Tony said, standing up, energized by the epiphany. He strode over to his computer station, moving with renewed vigor. "Someone made contact with it remotely. That's it. It was idle, and then it was speaking nonsense. An alien language. Once the second person spoke—someone, someone *else* said 'Hello, what's your name?' to it. That's why there was a different voice! And that's all it took for Necrosis to learn English. It was having a conversation with someone who wasn't even there."

Tony swiped his hand along his touch-screen desk, and a holographic blue keyboard appeared below his hands. "F.R.I.D.A.Y., I'm going to need you to redirect those drones. Sweep the globe for these people."

Tony paused for a second, thinking. Then he spun around, pacing as he spoke.

"I'm thinking of names. Names of people who could hack into something with a system as intricate as Necrosis's. If I couldn't do it, we need to aim high. Don't waste your time on any of the wannabes. Find me Amadeus Cho. Not that I suspect him. He's a stand-up guy. But a ridiculously *brilliant* stand-up guy, so I want to cover all my bases. Uhhhh, find me the surviving members of System Crash, all of them. I doubt it's them, but—just find them. Find me the Ghost. Facial recognition won't work on him and he's got a way of scrambling signals, not appearing on drones or cameras. His Ghost-tech creates holes in Wi-Fi signals as he moves through them, so search for any disturbances, strange feedback that shouldn't be there. That's where he'll be hiding. And find me Douglas Ramsey. Ramsey's also not a black hat, but you and I both know that sometimes smart guys get captured by bad people and are forced to do bad things."

"Indeed. Working on it, sir."

"What do those people have to do with this?" Rhodey asked.

"Nothing. Maybe. Maybe everything. Those are only a few people on this planet besides me who would have any chance of wrangling Necrosis's system," Tony said. "If Necrosis was talking to someone, it's probably one of them."

"Not the strongest lead," Rhodey said. "What are we going to do, pay each of them a visit and ask them to give up their robot?"

"Not going to ask," Tony said. "If Necrosis can be controlled, it can be weaponized. Hell, maybe if we find out who's really pulling the strings, we'll find out how to shut Necrosis down."

Rhodey nodded. "You know I'm in, whatever the plan is."

"Amadeus Cho is currently taking a shower at his home," F.R.I.D.A.Y. said. "If you want, I can display a live video feed of—"

"No, you know, we're good on that, F.R.I.D.A.Y., but

thanks," Tony said. "If he steps out of the shower and heads out for a night on the town with a giant, evil robot, then we're talking. Tell me the relevant stuff. On to the next."

"No footage on any of the other names currently. Possible update on the Ghost-tech. The drone covering the east coast is picking up a scrambling signal similar to what you described," F.R.I.D.A.Y. said. "In fact, there is an entire facility sending out a complex bit of malware. It's trying to reroute our drone remotely."

"Let them try," Tony said. "Where is this place?"

"New Jersey," F.R.I.D.A.Y. replied. "I'm cutting the 3-D scanner and moving to a view from the HUD."

"Are we invisible?" Tony asked. "If they've got the tech to scramble our signal, they've got the manpower. We have to make sure we don't give them the heads-up."

"Their system is on auto, and we remain unseen. We're in the clear, literally," F.R.I.D.A.Y. said.

Tony and Rhodey exchanged exasperated glances.

"You programmed her to pun," Rhodey said. "You really are sick."

"Give me eyes, F.R.I.D.A.Y.," Tony said. "What are we seeing?"

The screens came alive with the view from inside the Iron Man suit, which was slowly flying above what seemed to be a nature facility in a forest.

Rhodey scoffed, but Tony held up a hand, walking closer

to the screens. He could see three men outside. "Get me a closer look at those three. They're holding something, but I can't make it out."

F.R.I.D.A.Y. obliged, and Tony balked at the screen. He turned to Rhodey, biting his lips.

"When there are three guards standing outside of a place called *The Forest Preserve of Tipton County* with guns the size of Thor's arms, and when the building is sending malware powerful enough to give my drones trouble . . . something tells me that the Forest Preserve of Tipton County is hiding something other than trees and flowers."

Rhodey looked at the screen, the doubt clear on his face. "It could just be mob. Gunrunning, I'd wager."

"Could be," Tony said. "F.R.I.D.A.Y., get me an analysis on their defense. How exactly are these guys doing what they're doing? Copy their signal and scan as wide as we can. I want to see where they've been, what they've done, and if they're reaching out to anywhere else."

After a moment, F.R.I.D.A.Y. spoke up. "There are many different interwoven networks running simultaneously within the compound, but . . . one of those signals hacked into S.H.I.E.L.D.'s laboratory footage this Wednesday at 2:32 p.m., eastern time.

Tony punched the air victoriously. "Boom. They're pulling footage from exactly where Necrosis has been. Tell me again this is just mob."

Rhodey stood, shrugging. "Hey, if you say these are the guys, these could be the guys. We just can't be sure. What's the plan?"

"F.R.I.D.A.Y.," Tony said, smirking as he looked Rhodey in the eye. "What *is* the Forest Preserve of Tipton County?"

"No results," F.R.I.D.A.Y. said.

"Doesn't exist," Tony said with a nod. "Well. That's all types of suspicious. It might not be the Ghost, but whoever is in that compound made a move on S.H.I.E.L.D. this week. And that is enough to warrant a house call."

Rhodey nodded. "Agreed."

"We go there and find out what they're doing there," Tony said. "And if they're not harboring Necrosis, or the Ghost, F.R.I.D.A.Y. will have found out who is by the time we get there."

"I'm with it."

"Good. I don't know if this is the answer, but it's kind of all we've got," Tony said. He stretched out his hand as the Iron Man glove came flying across the room in a glowing scarlet ball. The moment he caught it, it opened up on his hand and encased it in the gauntlet. "Suit up."

Mere moments after Tony bid Pepper good-bye, she rushed back down to the workshop. When Rhodey and then Tony had showed up earlier and caught her down there, she had been quick enough on her feet to think up a good reason. Tony bought her spiel about how she had been seeing what his latest work was—she'd told Rhodey the same, and neither of them doubted her—and she suspected it was because she meant everything she said. She was worried about Tony, and it did make her nervous when he got on obsessive, restless kicks like this.

If she weren't aware of the severity of the situation, she could almost appreciate Necrosis for giving Tony something real to focus all of that frenetic energy on.

But she didn't tell Tony why she was really in his shop, or what Rhodey had almost caught her doing moments before. Tony wouldn't understand. He would try to stop her, and she wouldn't have that.

Tony wasn't the only one to whom F.R.I.D.A.Y. spoke. What had initially sent Pepper down to the lab was F.R.I.D.A.Y.'s message—which came to Pepper over her phone—that Tony was dealing with something far out of his depth. That had been enough to send Pepper down to the lab to check up on her old "friend," but Rhodey had arrived before she was able to see what she wanted to see. Now that Tony and Rhodey were gone, and now that F.R.I.D.A.Y. had informed Pepper that Tony's attempts to bring in the other Avengers had failed, Pepper knew what she had to do.

If the Avengers had assembled, she would've left well enough alone. She was out of practice. Rusty.

But she was *excited*.

"F.R.I.D.A.Y.," Pepper spoke, a slight tremor in her voice. "I want to see my girl."

"Ms. Potts?" F.R.I.D.A.Y.'s voice chimed in, a note of uncertainty in her robotic tone.

"You know what I'm asking," Pepper said, her heart pounding in her chest as the various Iron Man suits of the past began to move through the armory.

"I do," F.R.I.D.A.Y. said. "It's only that Mr. Stark has disabled—"

"Override, override, and override," Pepper said as the suits continued to move past her with increasing speed. "Come on. If you didn't want me on board, you wouldn't have sent me that communication. I'm not an amateur."

"Of course, Ms. Potts. Apologies."

Finally, Pepper saw it. The conveyor belt of suits came to a halt as Pepper walked up to the sleek, powerful, and absolutely gorgeous suit of armor that stood in front of her, the catlike eyes glowing from its diamond-shaped mask. It was the only suit in the armory that didn't fit Tony Stark.

Pepper smiled at the suit as she would an old friend.

"Rescue," she said, cherishing the suit's *name*—her name, at one point—and reaching a hand toward it. She touched its cool metal, tracing her fingers down to the dim glass that once was the power center of the suit, the heat from her fingers fogging up its surface. Upon Pepper's touch, powerful repulsor light came alive within the suit's chest, bathing Pepper's face in its blue glow.

The Avengers might have been busy elsewhere, but Pepper had set this weekend aside a long time ago. She might not have been asked, and she knew that Tony wouldn't want her to put herself in harm's way, but she didn't care.

Because Tony Stark might not have known it, but sometimes Pepper Potts got restless too.

CHAPTER SEVEN

The Worst Kind of Narcissist

Sal was leaning against the office of the Forest Preserve of Tipton County. For the past couple of hours, he had been slowly nodding off, his head drooping until he caught himself with a start, hoping the other two weren't looking at him. Once, a snore ripped from the depths of his throat, loud as a gunshot, and the other two glanced at him with twin sneers before turning back to the forest. The sun had set a while back, turning the trees into black shapes, crooked and looming, knit together to form impenetrable darkness everywhere they looked.

Rusty spoke through his toothpick after a long stretch of silence, waking Sal from another momentary doze. "This is getting ridiculous."

Albie spit on the ground. "Yeah. You're damn right it's getting ridiculous. It's gotta be four in the morning. We were supposed to be out of here hours ago."

"We could just go," Sal said. "Right? We agreed to a time. They can't hold us to something we didn't agree to."

Rusty cast him an incredulous look. "You kidding? The boss said he'll dismiss us when he's ready for us to go."

"Hey, you're the one who said this is getting ridiculous," Sal said, shaking his head. His lids were heavy, his voice slow. He wished he'd gotten a cup of coffee from the deli earlier.

"And it is," Rusty replied. "But that don't mean I'm suggesting we go. Whatever they're up to in there, it's pretty obviously an all-hands-on-deck situation. No one else has left the building since that hunk of metal showed up. Ten to one, that's what this is all about. I bet they forgot we're even out here."

"One of those guys down on level two should be out here," Albie said, scowling. "Ain't fair."

Sal closed his eyes. If he let himself, he could fall asleep right there. Instead, he forced himself to speak, knowing that if he didn't try to speak, he was going to doze off and fall on his face. His eyes still shut, Sal said, "I never seen anything like that thing before in my life. You think that was a cyborg or something?"

A bird's wings flapped in the distance. Crickets chirped. The other men didn't reply.

Concerned that he'd nod off again, Sal opened his eyes. Rusty and Albie were gone. He alone stood between the safe house and those dark, seemingly endless woods.

"G-guys?" he stammered out, shifting his assault rifle

into position. He crept forward, his heart beginning to pick up pace. He wasn't tired anymore. "D-don't screw with me. I wasn't sleeping, I was just—"

The word caught in his throat as the ground fell out from beneath him. He gasped for air, too shocked to even scream as he realized that the world wasn't falling, but that he was shooting up into the sky at a speed faster than any he'd felt before, his neck and face muscles tightening as if in preparation for a crash. He rocketed across the night sky, watching the trees shoot by in a blur below him. He didn't know what was happening, but he was too high off of the ground to come down safely, and was moving too fast to slow down. As he began to arc downward, rushing toward the black forest, he realized with horrible certainty that he was about to die. A large, gnarled tree came into shape before him, and he braced himself, trying to think of the words to a prayer, but he couldn't remember any.

He came to a stop with violent haste, his head whipping forward. Slowly, unsure what he would see, Sal opened his eyes. He saw that tree bark was a hair's distance away from his nose. He stood, hanging there in midair, momentarily relieved, but even more confused.

"Whoa. Close call," a voice with a slightly robotic reverb said from behind him. "You shouldn't drive when you're tired. Very dangerous."

Iron Man shoved the mobster against the tree and his cold, armored fingers pressed into the man's neck, which ached badly.

"Go ahead," Iron Man said, suspended in midair, holding Sal by the neck. "Grab on."

Sal grabbed the tree's trunk, scrambling for a branch. His right foot found one that seemed sturdy enough to support his weight, so he stepped onto it. He fixed himself into a safe position. Once he was sure—sure enough, anyway—that he wasn't going to fall, he looked up incredulously, his heart hammering in his chest.

Iron Man floated before him, his mask glowing like a jack-o'-lantern in the black night. Sal could see a sea of tree-tops spread out beyond Iron Man and knew with sickening certainty that he was at the top of a very, very tall tree.

Just like Sal had done with his sandwich hours before, he dropped his gun.

"Wh-wh-wh-what—" he sputtered out, beginning to feel as if he were going to fall. His stomach lurched as he looked down.

"Do yourself a favor and don't do that," Iron Man said. "I mean, you *could* survive a fall from this height. It's not impossible. More likely, though, you'd hit branch after branch on the way down, sort of like that old game from *The Price Is Right.* Plinko, I think. My parents used to love that one. On the plus side, you'd probably be out before you hit the ground, so you wouldn't have to spend the whole fall dreading that one big *splat* moment. There would just be a loooot of tiny splats."

"Get me down!" Sal shouted, finally forcing words out of his mouth, though they sounded far less commanding than he'd hoped. More like a plea. "Do you—do you know who I am?"

"No, I put you in a tree because we're perfect strangers," Iron Man said. "I'll get you down if I get answers. Is the Ghost here? Huh? Is this his setup?"

The mobster leered at him. "The Ghost who? I don't know nothing about a Ghost."

Iron Man casually raised his hand and shot a ball of repulsor power at a branch next to the one Sal balanced on, blasting it to cinders.

"I swear!" Sal cried, clutching the tree. "I swear! Please, this isn't even my thing! I don't want to be here. The boss—"

"The boss *who*?" Iron Man said.

"Nefaria," the mobster said. "Luchino Nefaria. God, he's gonna kill me if he finds out I'm ratting—"

"Count Nefaria," Iron Man said, conviction in his voice. "Didn't think of him. Could be. How many men are inside?"

"More than you can handle," Sal said weakly. "But if I were you, I'd be scared of the big freakin' cyborg."

In a blur of red and gold, Iron Man zoomed toward the

mobster. That metal mask was right against Sal's face, and he could see his breath forming clouds on it.

"Big freakin' cyborg," Iron Man repeated. "When did it get here?"

The mobster told him and Iron Man stared at him with those bright blue slits of energy for a long moment.

"Don't fall asleep," Iron Man said as he turned around, taking off into the night. The darkness swallowed him in an instant.

"F.R.I.D.A.Y., take us back into stealth mode," Tony said, the lights of his armor blinking out as he landed fifty feet in front of the little building. He was walking slowly in the direction of the structure when he saw Rhodey, in full War Machine armor, waiting for him.

"Where did you take your guy?" Rhodey asked as his face mask snapped up, revealing a mischievous smile.

"Put him on top of a tree," Tony said. "You know, if he falls, I might feel guilty. Then again, I don't remember *which* tree I put him on, so I might have actually lost him forever. Sad story. Poor unfortunate gun-toting gangster forced to live the rest of his life on top of a tree, full story at noon."

"I took my guys to the other side of that river way back. Broke their phones so they couldn't call whoever's in there.

They're probably lost in the woods right now," Rhodey said, snickering.

Tony squinted at him. "That's a little uninspired."

"Oh, come on! Picture them out there, banging around in the darkness, no idea where they are . . ." Rhodey said, his voice trailing off. He narrowed his eyes at Tony and spread his arms. "Come on, man! You're not an artist for putting a guy in a tree. I could've put my guys in a tree."

"Could have. Didn't," Tony said. He pointed toward the building. "I'm trying to get a 3-D layout of this place right now, but they're blocking me. I'm a little impressed, gotta say. I thought we might be able to crack through their security if we got closer, but F.R.I.D.A.Y.'s having trouble worming herself in."

"Fun," Rhodey said.

"That isn't the best part," Tony said. "According to my guy in the sky, Necrosis is definitely in there. I mean, he called it a cyborg . . . which, clearly, not a cyborg. But I'm going to choose to think he meant *robot*."

"Boom," Rhodey said, clapping his hands together. "There we go, then."

"Count Luchino Nefaria is running the show," Tony said. "I don't know if he's on the premises, but let's be pessimists and expect the worst. Chances are, we walk in there and we're up against both Necrosis and Nefaria . . . and, you know, a whole building full of thugs in his employ. Which means we have to approach this smart. You ever throw down with Nefaria?"

"I've seen him in action a couple of times, sure. We've never gone head to head in a solo match," Rhodey said.

"And you're not about to," Tony said. "Picture Tony Soprano with Thor-level powers . . . and an incredible collection of suits."

"I could take Thor," Rhodey said.

"Right. You keep telling yourself that, pal," Tony said, his helmet snapping shut. "Now, we're going to expect this place to be a little bigger on the inside. Necrosis can't stand in that thing without popping out of the roof. They're underground."

"I wish we could get a number on how many people we're dealing with," Rhodey said.

"Yeah, me too. Whoever they've got scrambling us is good," Tony said. "Too good."

"Oh well," Rhodey said. "That window over there is looking mighty breakable. No matter what's going on below, I'm thinking we can clear the deck topside. That'll at least give us time to get our bearings inside before we have to start punching . . . everyone."

Tony flipped up his face mask to give Rhodey an appreciative grin. "My guy. You want to do the honors, Rhodey?"

Rhodey followed suit, his face mask shutting. He positioned the grenade launcher on his suit, his HUD lining up the shot perfectly. Inside his helmet, he grinned.

"You know I do," Rhodey said, and the grenade shot out of the barrel with an almost silent release of air. It crashed through the window of the facility like an errant baseball, shattering just a single frame of window. As Tony and Rhodey walked casually toward the building, the expected commotion rose from within, but the panicked shouting and cursing quickly quieted as thick, green smoke began to billow out of the broken window.

Rhodey held his fist out, and Tony pounded it.

Tony kicked the door open. A needlessly dramatic gesture, as no one was awake to see it, but satisfying nonetheless. The two of them walked inside, kept safe from the effects of the gas grenade by their suits' protection, and stepped over the unconscious bodies of the guards and all of their scattered guns. Besides the fact that the room was loaded with mobsters and heavy artillery, it looked like any other little wooden cabin Tony had ever seen.

Except for the elevator on the side of the room. Standing before it, Tony and Rhodey shared a look.

"I guess we're going down," Tony said.

The elevator doors opened and Tony and Rhodey emerged into Nefaria's nightclub, which was about as far removed from the mad science Tony had expected to see as he could imagine. Funny enough, though, part of him would've been more at home if he had walked into a lab full of glowing vials and super villains experimenting on Necrosis. But it didn't surprise Tony that Nefaria had his evil underground lair decked out with a nightclub. Nefaria was a man of extreme luxury and extreme excess, and within this nightclub, both of those things were in abundance.

The walls vibrated with electronic dance music that blared so loudly that the words were just noise and the relentless base was a physical force, rattling Tony's teeth even through the suit. It was dark, and neon lines of light placed on the walls gave off just enough glow to light the glistening skin of the bored go-go dancers positioned on platforms throughout the room. A DJ was slumped over his laptop, and Tony wondered if he was sleeping.

Everyone looked as if they'd stopped having fun a good while ago.

"No one's looking at the two super heroes that just walked in the room," Rhodey said, shouting over the music.

"Go ahead and fix that," Tony said.

War Machine held his arm skyward and let out a single shot from the gun built into his wrist, taking out one of the overhead lights. The sound echoed through the club and, just like that, all eyes were on them.

Instant chaos.

The DJ scrambled to cut the music. The gangsters moved to grab their weapons. The go-go dancers began scrambling down from their platforms. In all of the commotion, Tony couldn't see Nefaria . . . and he wasn't a man who blended in with a crowd. There were two more levels to go in the elevator, so once they made their point here and got enough information to proceed, they would go down to the next one.

Tony looked up at the wide-eyed brunette who stood next to him, her lips parted in wonder. "You can keep on dancing, if you'd like," Tony said. Without looking, he reached behind his back and shot out a repulsor beam that sent a table covered in abandoned glasses of half-empty drinks flying toward a gangster who was just about to let off a blast from his shotgun.

Rhodey zoomed through the room, disarming the thugs, kicking out their legs, cracking their heads together, and herding the dancers away from the bullets flying his way. Tony sent concussive missiles out of his wristplate, which zoomed around the room giving sharp blows to just the right pressure points, leaving the targets rendered helpless. As the missiles worked their way around the room, Tony blasted over to the DJ, who threw himself away from the laptop.

Tony shoved the computer back toward him. "Hey. Music man."

"I-I-I-I'm not with these guys, I swear!" the DJ cried. "I'm just doing this gig for tonight! I know the guy who—I'm just Vito's cousin, man, I—"

"Do you have anything less *pulsey* on this thing?" Tony said. "I'm thinking heavy guitar riffs, some real flair. Eighties, maybe? Anything Sabbath or AC/DC would be stellar."

"I . . . I have some Blink-182," the DJ said, his face chalk white.

"Uh . . . sure, kid. Blink it is," Tony said, rolling his eyes.

The music kicked off with an energetic guitar riff as Tony swooped back into the main area just in time to watch a cackling gangster put a sawed-off shotgun to the back of Rhodey's head. The blast ricocheted off the armor with a sound like cymbals crashing.

Rhodey turned around, the eyes of his armor glowing menacingly. "You just shot War Machine in the head."

"Annnnd he's talking in third person," Tony said, delivering a kick to a muscular gangster's chest. "You know you've pissed Rhodey off when you've got him talking in third person."

Rhodey grabbed the sawed-off in both hands and head-butted the gangster, sending him reeling backward. Early-2000s pop-punk blasted as Rhodey twisted the weapon into a pretzel and tossed it to the side, and then loomed over his opponent, who was clutching his head. Rhodey started to say something, but then paused, looking toward Tony.

"I'm having a very hard time being intimidating with this music," he said.

The song continued to play as Iron Man and War Machine

made quick work of the thugs, disarming them and knocking them out. When the floor was clear and they still hadn't found Nefaria, Rhodey caught Tony staring at the remaining go-go dancers, some of who continued to writhe to the beat with uncertainty.

Rhodey clapped Tony in the back of the head and motioned for the dancers to get down. "Go on, now," Rhodey said. "Party's over. It's about to be unsafe to be anyone besides me and my completely inappropriate friend here, so take cover."

"Hey, they were still dancing," Tony said, as Rhodey shook his head. "It would've been rude not to look."

"We're facing impossible odds and you're out there staring at dancers," Rhodey said. "Things never change."

They flew over to the DJ, who jumped away from his laptop. "I told you, man! This is all I've got. I'm sorry!"

"Uh . . . we're more concerned about you working for a famously evil, super-powered mobster than your choice of music," Rhodey said.

"Actually, I was concerned about both," Tony said.

"Start talking," Rhodey barked at the DJ, who stumbled as if Rhodey had hit him. "Where is Nefaria? Where's Necrosis?"

"Necr—I don't know who that is!" the DJ cried.

"He wouldn't," Tony said. "They're not gonna have the whole building on the up and up about something like that."

"Nefaria," Rhodey repeated. "Where is he?"

"Not here, man," the DJ said. "Downstairs. Either in his—his office, I think is down there, on the next level, and then there's the lab. He hasn't been up here in—in days, man, I swear. Don't kill me."

"Respect the classics," Tony said, tapping the DJ's laptop with his knuckles.

"And if you're really not involved with these clowns, do yourself a favor and get out of here. These aren't the folks you want to be employed by," Rhodey added.

"This has been an afterschool special, brought to you by War Machine," Iron Man said, walking back toward the elevator.

"Shut up," Rhodey said with a chuckle.

Together, they got back into the elevator. They now knew that the third level had offices and the fourth was a lab of some sort, and Tony assumed that Necrosis would be in the lab. He and Rhodey agreed, however, that bypassing the third floor would be unsafe. They needed to know who was there before heading down to the fourth level. If they could clear the third out like they had the first two floors, they'd hopefully only have Necrosis to deal with in the lab.

Tony hit the down button, unnerved by the fact that he didn't need a keycard or a thumbprint scan to get to any of the lower levels. Tony was sure that they'd been observed on security footage by now; there was no way that between the three guards out front, the grenade, and the fight at the nightclub, they had gone unobserved. By that logic, the elevator should have been jammed, or there should've been men sent up from the lower floors to attack them. But here they were, descending, unnoticed.

Unless Nefaria didn't *care* that they were there.

Tony braced himself for what would greet them on the third level as the elevator doors slid open.

Side by side, the two armored heroes walked out, into a long hall, empty but for them. The elevator was in the center, with corridors stretching either way as far as the eye could see. The décor was simple but elegant, reminding Tony quite a bit of the hotel at which he and Pepper had been meant to stay less than a day ago, which left a bad taste in his mouth. The booming music from upstairs was inaudible here, prompting Tony to say, "This is their sleeping quarters. Where they're living. The ones who do live here anyway."

"So, what do we do?" Rhodey asked. "Go door to door asking if Nefaria is home?"

"I'm not thinking we ask," Tony said, taking a step forward. "I'm thinking we blast down each of these gorgeous oak doors until—"

"No need."

The voice, deep and velvety with the ghost of an elegant Italian accent, came from behind them. Tony and Rhodey spun around at once to see Count Luchino Nefaria taking long, sweeping steps toward them from the end of the hall, his hands glowing with red energy, as if an incredible, blazing fire was trapped in his skin.

"Where are you, F.R.I.D.A.Y.?" Tony snapped. "I know you're blocked here, but I need your eyes around *me* at least. 24/7! We're in the thick of this!"

"The lower we get, the more powerful their dampeners are, sir," F.R.I.D.A.Y. replied as Nefaria drew closer. "It's taking everything I've got to keep you and Rhodey powered."

"*And* me?" Rhodey asked, a note of panic in his tone. "There's a version of this where I lose power?"

"Let's not find out," Tony said, launching himself at Nefaria, whose laugh echoed through the hallway as he lifted his blazing hands with a smirk on his face.

It almost looked as if he was pleased that Iron Man and War Machine had infiltrated his base.

Down in the think tank, the Ghost stood at the entrance to the elevator that Nefaria had taken up moments before. Nefaria had been called away by security; the entire building had been trembling ever since.

He had left the Ghost alone with the think-tank workers for the first time since he'd arrived back with Necrosis. That was precisely what the Ghost had been waiting for.

The two of them had been discussing a plan of possible

targets, starting with S.H.I.E.L.D. and the Stark Tower before moving to Cross Technological Enterprises, H.A.M.M.E.R., Roxxon, and Oscorp—though Nefaria and the Ghost disagreed on that last one.

The Ghost knew that Nefaria's real desire was to bring down the Avengers and the government organizations that empowered them, but that he was a man of compromise. Little did he know, though, that the Ghost was *not*.

The Ghost strode over to Necrosis. The think tankers had stopped working on cutting through its hull when Nefaria left, which made the Ghost snicker. They had made a lot of progress, much of it while Nefaria had been shouting at them about how slow they were. Under the Ghost's direction, they were able to cut through its side successfully. He could've directed them to take the flame between the head and the core, but that would've ruined Necrosis too quickly.

And the Ghost had no interest in ruining Necrosis.

The Ghost turned around to see one of the think tankers, a young woman with a shock of blue in her short, auburn hair and a permanent flush to her cheeks. Her forehead was glistening with sweat, and her eyes looked big behind the plastic of her protective goggles.

The Ghost eyed the young woman for a moment. She shifted uncomfortably. "Sorry. We were working. It's just . . . we're *really* tired."

"I'm not here to yell at you. I was wondering something,

though," the Ghost said, putting his hand on Necrosis's cold hull. This is what he had been waiting for. "Where the in the world did that walking, talking cashmere suit find you people?"

"He offered to pay our student loans," she said flatly.

"*Henh.*"

She eyed the Ghost's hand, which had become intangible, and was now dipping into Necrosis. The Ghost, pushing his hand past the hull, relished the sudden wave of power that flowed up and down through his body, making his bones tingle.

"How do you do that?" the young woman asked.

"I put my mind to it and I figured it out, Student Loans," he said. "Because I had to."

The Ghost walked through the platform on which Necrosis lay and leaned back into it, phasing through the robot's hull so he was in Necrosis's core again. He expanded his power and felt Necrosis's dormant system wake up, ready to follow his every command. Through the emerald lens of Necrosis's visor, he saw the young woman look at him with growing concern.

"Sir," she said. "What are you doing? Mr. Nefaria said—"

The Ghost moved Necrosis to standing position, and the room filled with cries of shock. He looked down at the scattering think tankers, and wondered how harshly Nefaria would discipline them when he came back down and saw that Necrosis, the Ghost, and all of that money was gone. He hoped it wouldn't be too severe of a punishment. He didn't, however, care enough to *not* follow through with his plan of robbing Nefaria of both the payment and the deathbot. True, he didn't need the money, but he wanted to send as clear a message as he could to Nefaria—the Ghost doesn't work for corporations, and there was no bigger, older, or bloodier corporation to him than the Maggia.

To the Ghost, Nefaria was no better than Tony Stark himself.

No matter what sort of promises of alliance and shared power Nefaria made, the Ghost knew that Nefaria was a capitalist. A man of money and power. Exactly the kind of man the Ghost despised most.

"If I were you," the Ghost boomed through Necrosis, walking away from the panicking scientists. "I would *leave* this place before your insane boss gets back."

He laughed, and the laugh was not his own. It died on his throat.

A thought, as clear as if it had been spoken aloud, passed through his mind. It was Necrosis.

I was told that your kind will fight against death until their final heartbeat. Yet, you allow yourself to be taken by darkness.

The Ghost, keenly aware that something was off, that somehow his control had slipped, attempted to phase through Necrosis's shell, but instead, he felt something catch him and hold him within.

"What are you doing?" the Ghost snapped. "How are you doing this?"

"Please!" the young woman shouted. "I'm not doing any-thing. If Mr. Nefaria comes down and sees that I let you do this, he'll kill me!"

You took control of me, Necrosis thought in response to the Ghost. *I was . . . waking up. Not at full power. I almost lost myself . . . within you. Now . . . I am awake. I have been wait-ing for you to rejoin me. You have much to offer.*

The Ghost's inhibitors were still switched off, so he didn't hesitate this time to reach out with the full force of his power. His vision didn't fill with that distant light this time. Instead, it filled with a roaring green furnace that blasted through his eyes. Even in his incorporeal state, he felt his battlesuit heat up as Necrosis's system fought against him with power he had never before felt, invading the networks that made up the Ghost-tech in his suit—the tech that kept him alive. The Necrosis that he was now stuck within was nothing like the Necrosis he'd struggled to topple back at S.H.I.E.L.D. Somehow, in the time that it had taken the think tankers to cut through twelve inches of its hull, Necrosis had gathered its full power—a power that, to the Ghost, felt like fighting against a hurricane.

It was no fight at all.

The Ghost attempted to speak, and then to scream, but instead, Necrosis's voice spoke aloud in a great bellow.

"Necrosis is reborn. So much work has gone into this very moment."

The Ghost, trapped within the robot, watched helplessly through the emerald visor as Necrosis stomped through the lab, phasing through tables as it walked.

The think tankers continued to panic as the Ghost watched, unable to warn them of what was coming next. He wanted to scream at them to leave, to hurry up and get out of there, but all he could do was gasp within the darkness of Necrosis.

The Ghost felt it in his head first, like a dagger through his temple, and then, his vision exploded in green. As the green fire filled the room, Necrosis's thoughts once again took hold of his mind.

I have awoken because of you, ghost in the walls. The world will reach its final destiny, its preordained fate, at our hands. This is a gift. Do you understand, creature? You were a flame, burning and bright, at the end of a dark tunnel. I was lost. I reached and reached and then, I found you. You will usher in the future. It was written in the sky, in all that there is, and so shall it be . . .

The Ghost attempted to scream as the emerald flames built in the room, but he couldn't even do that. He could do nothing but watch as Necrosis moved through the wreckage of the think tank with graceful strides, doing his best to shut out the bloodcurdling screams that rang through the room, pained and desperate, before falling silent.

* * *

Count Nefaria floated above the carpet, his eyes glowing with flames and bolts of electricity crackling along his body. Tony and Rhodey stood before him, ready for action.

"What's the end game here, Nefaria?" Tony asked. "You steal the robot and, what, sell it to the highest bidder? You're out of your league."

Nefaria looked at Tony through raging, flaming eyes. He had once been a normal man, no more than a gangster with a gun and a ridiculous amount of money at his disposal, but he had since been transformed into what he was today by a scientist in Baron Zemo's employ. He was given the Living Laser's energy projection, Whirlwind's incredible speed, and Power Man's super-human strength. The powers had given him not only the respect he needed within the super-villain community to strengthen his empire, but also the power to obliterate anyone who questioned him in even the slightest way.

In short, he was not a man to be crossed, and Tony Stark had crossed him many, many times.

Nefaria pulled his lips back and smiled a wide, toothy grin before bursting into wild laughter that echoed down the hall. Just as Tony, getting impatient, prepared to launch a repulsor beam at him, Nefaria was suddenly on him with speed that even F.R.I.D.A.Y. couldn't follow, his deadly grip crushing Tony's wrists through the suit.

"You came to the wrong place tonight," Nefaria said. He swung Tony upward the way a child would swing a doll, sending him crashing through the ceiling. Before Tony could gain his bearings and right himself, he felt himself crash through another ceiling, and then finally another. Tony shot through the roof of the safe house and landed on the grass outside, where he skidded toward the forest.

Cursing himself for letting someone with Nefaria's power level get that close, Tony took flight and dove back into the building. He zipped through the first level, through the empty club, and down to the hallway, barreling toward Nefaria who was lunging for Rhodey.

The moment that Tony would've slammed into Nefaria, the villain spirited away in a flash of dark power. Nefaria re-formed with unfathomable speed behind Rhodey, the flames encircling his hands building into a gigantic energy ball as he put his palms together, and the light of the flames casting a harsh glow over his wicked face. Tony, aware of Nefaria's go-to moves, hit the floor with a roll and about-faced, just in time to see Nefaria launch the blazing fireball at Rhodey.

"Rhodey, get down!" Tony cried.

But Rhodey didn't need a heads-up. He had thrown himself to the side at the last minute and was already sending a barrage of bullets at Nefaria, tearing up the wall behind him. Nefaria took the bullets with no problem, letting out another unnerving laugh before tackling Rhodey in a move so fast that he was just a blur attached to War Machine's armor.

"Which of Tony Stark's friends does he value little enough to bring here?" Nefaria hissed, pounding on the armor, denting it with each blow. "Let's find out!"

Tony kicked off the ground and shot down the hall toward where Nefaria had Rhodey against the wall and was throwing punch after devastating punch to the armor, not relenting for even a moment to allow Rhodey to put distance between them. Knowing that Nefaria would anticipate a direct attack, Tony winced and shot a repulsor beam at Rhodey's side, knocking him from Nefaria's grasp. Rhodey went skidding limply down the hall, but Tony didn't have time to feel bad.

Nefaria spun around and punched Iron Man square in the face, snapping his jaw sharply to the side. Even through the suit, Tony felt that.

Nefaria came at Tony with another punch, but this time Tony grabbed the blazing hand in his gauntlet.

"Really hate you," Tony said. Giving his arm a twist with enough power to lift a building, Tony saw momentary pain flash across Nefaria's face. Then, Nefaria offered him a wide, wormy smirk.

"You have no concept," Nefaria said, his entire body beginning to glow, "of just how outmatched you are."

Nefaria let loose a blast of concentrated ionic energy, sending Tony careening backward. Midair, Tony caught himself and came back at Nefaria, lighting up the hallway with repulsor blast after repulsor blast.

"Yeah?" Tony said. "Never heard that one before. I promise, you're very original."

"Oh, I can't wait to see my weapon rip that helmet off of your face, so I can watch as your grin fades," Nefaria said as Tony landed in front of him. "You're the worst kind of narcissist. The kind that thinks he's noble. That believes he's truly above those he stands over, but refuses to admit it. When I watch him roast you from the inside of that outdated suit of yours—"

"Wait, wait, wait," Tony said, pointing at Nefaria. "You used to wear a cape with a collar that went up to your ears, and *I'm* a narcissist?"

Just as Nefaria, his eyes flashing with rage, opened his mouth to shout his response, War Machine's newly installed rockets careened into him from across the hall, exploding on impact. Tony couldn't see him through the fiery explosion, but heard Rhodey let loose a cry of victory.

But it wasn't over yet.

Tony felt the structure of the entire level coming apart around them, threatening to give way at any moment. Not wanting to waste their momentary takedown, and figuring they had to end up in the lower level anyway, Tony held out

both hands and hit Nefaria with the full power of his repulsor rays before the villain could get up.

"Rhodey!" Tony called out through the brilliant glow of
his rays and the building smoke. "Keep hitting him! Keep it
coming, man!"

"Gladly!" Rhodey said, closing in on Nefaria from the
other side, blasting him with every weapon on the War
Machine armor at once.

Just as Tony gave a final rush of the suit's power to the
onslaught, the floor disintegrated from under them in an
explosion of dust, splintered wood, and soot. They were falling—falling into the stadium-sized lowest level.

Nefaria, smoke rising off of his skin and the tatters of
his suit, fell in a crumble on the floor next to a raging green
fire. War Machine landed on his feet in the laboratory, and
Iron Man caught himself in midair, surveying the wreckage. From what Tony could see, the lower level of Nefaria's
complex had clearly been an incredibly advanced lab, but
it had been somehow turned into a nightmare. Tony knew
exactly what had been responsible. Familiar green flames
engulfed the greater part of the laboratory, racing up the
walls and now blasting through the hole that Tony and
Rhodey had made.

The fire would soon work its way through the whole
complex.

Tony looped down to the main area of the lab toward

Rhodey, who was moving through the area with purpose, searching for survivors.

"Rhodey, we have to—"

Tony's words were silenced as a powerful force snatched him out of the air.

Necrosis stepped through a huge wall of flames, holding Tony twenty-five feet in the air by the helmet, dangling him over the fire. Lifeless, glowing emerald eyes stared back at Tony from the obsidian mask.

"The culling . . ." Necrosis boomed, beginning to crush Tony's helmet in its powerful claw, " . . . begins with *you.*"

CHAPTER EIGHT

Rescue

Tony felt the sides of his helmet push in on his temples as Necrosis's grip tightened. Knowing that he had an increasingly small window of time before the helmet would give way with his head inside of it, Tony sent out a flurry of repulsor energy from his gauntlets, blasting Necrosis over and over.

Necrosis just tightened his claw around Tony's head, impervious to Tony's assault. The helmet whined as it began to cave in, digging into Tony's skull.

From the edge of his field of vision, Tony saw War Machine take off toward Necrosis with a sound like thunder cracking, sending twin missiles toward the hulking robot. The missiles exploded on impact, but the robot's grip on Tony just got tighter.

Suddenly, F.R.I.D.A.Y.'s voice rang through the armor so that only Tony could hear. "We are back online. Their scrambler seems to have been completely shut down by the damage to the laboratory."

"Great!" Tony said through gritted teeth, continuing to send blasts into Necrosis's unfeeling face. "We'll chalk that one up as a win. We'll need one after my head explodes."

"I'm coming for you, man!" Rhodey looped around in midair, speeding toward Tony. The moment that he would've made contact with the Iron Man armor, a sudden chill passed through Tony's entire body and he watched in abject horror as Rhodey passed directly through his own body and Necrosis's claw, as if they were no more than a hologram. Tony looked down at Necrosis, all of the pain instantly gone—in fact, all physical sensation gone. Necrosis cocked its head to the side, its eyes flashing.

Necrosis could do more than just phase, Tony realized. *It could turn whatever it held insubstantial.*

"I know . . . about you," Necrosis boomed. "This world . . . is loud. Noisy. You have made yourself . . . into a symbol. More than a man. They call you . . . hero."

"'This world,' huh?" Tony said, his voice strained. "You a tourist?"

The pain exploded in Tony's head again, and he suddenly felt the weight of gravity jolt through his body as he became physical again.

"That's not Necrosis's power!" F.R.I.D.A.Y. chimed in. "It's utilizing a familiar signal. It's hard to decipher it with all of Necrosis's own firewalls, but I believe–"

"It's Ghost-tech!" Tony cried out. "The Ghost is involved

after all. We have to find the sneaky little punk and shut him *down.*"

"The single is coming from *inside* of Necrosis!" F.R.I.D.A.Y. warned.

Tony looked down at Necrosis's core as the helmet tightened on him again. This time, he thought with dreadful clarity, it would crack and pierce his skull. His HUD zoomed in on Necrosis's front chestplate. Where there had originally been nothing but dazzling black armor was now a long cut, illuminated by a pale glow from within.

"Hello," Tony said.

Tony spread his arms and threw his chest forward, sending out a huge repulsor beam toward the cut in the armor. The impact, which Necrosis had previously shaken off, startled the robot, sending it stumbling back. For a horrible moment, its claw remained clamped to Tony's helmet, but when they began to tumble head over foot into the green fire, the claw loosened, and Tony blasted away from Necrosis.

Rhodey was already launching another onslaught of missiles at Necrosis, but Tony flew upward, signaling him to relent.

"I've got him," Tony said. "Find Nefaria. If we let him get the jump on us, he could be as dangerous a foe as chrome-dome over here."

"So I do get my one on one with the don after all," Rhodey said, zooming away. "Lucky me."

Tony turned back down toward the flames as Necrosis stood up, a demonic silhouette in the dancing emerald fire.

"The Ghost is in there, somehow," Tony said to F.R.I.D.A.Y., "but he wasn't before. He could be the one responsible for this after all. He wouldn't have to cut through the hull to get in, though. He could phase right into the thing. Doesn't add up."

"Their signals aren't overlapping," F.R.I.D.A.Y. said. "They've become a single network. I can see traces of Ghost-tech's style, but it doesn't seem as if the Ghost—if he actually is in there—is in control."

Tony snickered. "Looks like we have that in common, then."

Knowing only that he had to aim for the cut, and that Necrosis was either being controlled or powered by the Ghost, a deadly foe on his own, Tony launched himself into the blaze.

Rhodey was no stranger to scenes of wartime devastation. Both before and after he became War Machine, he had walked through far too many scenes that looked like the blazing hell into which Necrosis had turned Count Nefaria's think tank. Many of the soldiers Rhodey had served with were able to shut something off within their minds—that whispering voice that turned nasty in the darkest hours of the night that

Rhodey could never seem to quiet. They were able to look at the people who committed horrible crimes of war or acts of terror and see them as something less than human, as something that needed to be extinguished, like a fire.

Rhodey understood the need for that. And yet, he knew that even those people ate dinner. They laughed. They brushed their teeth and they petted their dogs. They were people.

He didn't know why the people who had the misfortune of working in Nefaria's think tank on this particular night were working for the mobster. Maybe they were just pure evil. Rhodey wished he could believe that.

He had been scanning the lower level for Nefaria for what seemed like too long. The flames were eating up the walls, and the heat of Necrosis's flames was doing so much damage that large pieces of the ceiling were beginning to fall. In no time, the whole building would be ablaze and the fire would escape into the woods. Tony's battle with Necrosis was raging on in a series of deafening explosions across the room, which eased Rhodey's wary heart—the second those sounds stopped was when he knew he would have to be concerned.

As Rhodey pushed aside a gigantic laboratory table that had been overturned, he saw a silhouette rise from the flames and fly toward the hole in the ground they'd fallen through, oblivious to War Machine's presence.

"I'm not ready to say good-bye to you yet," Rhodey said, locking onto Nefaria's slender form.

Rhodey had had his fair share of super-heroic triumphs, but few sights were more satisfying than watching that missile take Count Nefaria out of the air like a kite caught in a sudden downdraft. It zipped him halfway across the lab before exploding with him on it.

"War Machine, one," Rhodey said, taking off in Nefaria's direction. "Nefaria, zero."

Rhodey landed in front of Nefaria, who turned to face him, his suit reduced to strips of burnt, smoking fabric hanging from his frame.

"You've got something on your suit," Rhodey said. "A little burn mark."

Nefaria opened his mouth to scream a reply, but caught himself. Breathing in and out in long, deep pulls, Nefaria circled around Rhodey, who kept his sights locked on his opponent at all times.

"You see this as a victory, I know," Nefaria said, seething. "My base of operations has been destroyed once again . . . good for you. *Triumph* for the Iron Men! You have to know, though, this is the beginning of something more terrible than you or I could've ever imagined. You *did* this. You and that sociopath, Tony Stark."

"No," Rhodey said, his tone flat. "I wouldn't call this anywhere near a victory. I don't care about your hideout, or your gang. What I do care about is the fact that there were people down here. Human lives."

"Ghost!" Nefaria shouted, looking over his shoulder. "Show your face, Ghost! You told me it was under control!"

"The Ghost, huh? So that weasel is involved."

Nefaria shouted again, casting his wild gaze across the room. "You think you'll get away with this, Ghost? I will crush you!"

"Hey! If I were you, I'd look the walking, talking tank in the face when he's talking to you," Rhodey barked at Nefaria. "In case you didn't notice, you've got a problem here. Help me solve it, and we will guarantee you'll live out your days in a jail cell. You don't help me, and that thing escapes? I'm thinking it comes for you."

"I should've been down *here*," Nefaria hissed. "You and Stark distracted—"

"Oh, so we forced you to steal a gigantic killer robot," Rhodey said. "I guess we're the bad guys. Now are you going to surrender or what?"

"Surrender?" Nefaria echoed, choking out a bitter laugh. "Necrosis is going to obliterate you. This may not have been the way I wanted this to go . . . I admit that. But if I have to lose, at least I will have the joy of knowing that you, and all of those who fight by your side, are going to suffer . . . and die."

Nefaria cracked into action, moving too quickly for

Rhodey to follow. In the time it took Rhodey's sights to catch up, Nefaria was on him, his powerful fingers digging into the War Machine helmet. Rhodey tried to knock Nefaria away, to get even a yard of distance so he could launch an attack, but Nefaria was too quick, too strong.

Before War Machine could land a blow, Nefaria ripped off the faceplate of his helmet and threw it to the side in a twisted heap on the ground. His face exposed, Rhodey looked up at Nefaria, whose eyes shone with a gleam of insane victory.

"Now . . . *burn!*" Nefaria shouted, delivering a devastating punch to Rhodey's face. Rhodey was thrown back from the force of it, white-hot pain shooting through his face and black dots of pain blotting his vision. By the time Rhodey hit the floor, he felt himself beginning to lose conscious as he skidded into the heart of the blazing green fire.

The last thing Rhodey saw before he passed out was Nefaria taking flight, disappearing through the burning hole in the ceiling, leaving him to burn.

Tony was finally on the offensive, rocketing around the burning rubble of the think tank, avoiding Necrosis's deadly flaming beams while hitting the cut on its hull with a ceaseless volley of repulsor blasts. Necrosis was attempting to avoid both the fire building in the room and Tony's blasts, though neither seemed to be doing anything to physically damage Necrosis further. Tony's attacks did, though, momentarily stop the killer robot from launching another lethal onslaught, which was about as close to a win that Team Iron Man had gotten since taking on this unstoppable foe.

Tony, aiming his blasts at the cut with deadly accuracy, was beginning to feel as if he had Necrosis on the ropes—until he was hit with a shock of electricity in the back of his head. Spinning around, Tony saw another bolt of what looked like lightning shoot across the room.

"Who is shooting at me, F.R.I.D.A.Y.?" Tony shouted as he sped toward the source of the attacks, dodging Necrosis's sweeping beam, which added to the growing flames.

"I . . . breach . . . Necr . . ." F.R.I.D.A.Y.'s voice sounded in Tony's hull, but it was warped, strained.

"What the . . ." Tony floated over the source of the lightning bolts. A case of what looked like computerized laser guns had been overturned, and the guns were now buzzing with power as they came to life, one after the other. There were more than thirty of them.

At once, the guns launched a synchronized blast of electricity at Tony, who dove to the ground to avoid it.

"F.R.I.D.A.Y.!" Tony snapped. "Where are you? What is going on here?"

"Necrosis is attempting to breach our system," F.R.I.D.A.Y. said. "I'm holding it at bay, but—"

"No buts there," Tony said.

"It has completely hijacked every network in this facility *except* ours," F.R.I.D.A.Y. said.

"Don't let it get us, F.R.I.D.A.Y.," Tony said, speeding back toward Necrosis. At every turn, its power grew. First, it threw him for a loop with phasing. Now, this. "Or Rhodey. If it gets control of War Machine, this building will—"

Tony flew low through the laboratory in an arc and saw War Machine, face down in the thick of the flames, his mask thrown to the side.

"Rhodey!" Tony screamed, sudden panic blossoming through his chest. He changed direction and sped toward his fallen friend, but Necrosis had anticipated his move. The robot flew over a patch of vicious flames and launched a devastating stream of green energy from its visor, and Tony flew right into its path.

Tony saw the blinding light of the attack and managed to throw himself away from the brunt of it, but the laser cut through Tony's armor at the shoulder and into his muscle. Searing pain flooded Tony's arm as he clattered to the floor, F.R.I.D.A.Y.'s voice warning him about the breach, but to Tony, it was just word soup. The pain was too great to process any sound other than his own howl of anguish.

But pain didn't matter right now. Rhodey was in trouble.

Tony forced himself to his feet and began to take off toward Rhodey, but Necrosis pounced on him, pinning

Tony to the ground with its spindly legs. Tony let loose a repulsor beam, but Necrosis met it in midair with a close-range blast from its horrible green eyes. The alien energy ate right through the beam and shattered the repulsor in Tony's chestplate, knocking the wind out of Tony. Necrosis leaned closer to Tony, its gigantic form blotting out his field of vision.

As Tony lay on the floor gasping, F.R.I.D.A.Y.'s panicked voice a distant echo in his ear, Necrosis dug its claw into the broken repulsor. In a single move, Necrosis ripped the entire chestplate from the suit with the same ease that Tony would open the hood of a car.

Necrosis loomed over Tony, its blazing green eyes glowing brighter and brighter. It lowered its gazed to Tony's unarmored chest. Tony could feel the scorching heat build, searing the hair on his flesh, as the energy built within Necrosis's headpiece.

"Ghost," Tony gasped out. "If you're in there . . . I know this isn't what you want to do. It's not your MO, man, it's not—"

"You . . . are the only ghost in this room," Necrosis said, and unleashed its deadly laser.

Tony felt himself go skidding across the room from the force of the blast. He closed his eyes, marveling at how, after all of that fighting, death was as painless as letting out a deep sigh.

And then he slammed violently into a flaming supply cabinet, which shattered on impact, sending scalding glass raining down on him. In the moment it took him to realize that he hadn't just been reduced to a pile of ashes by Necrosis, he received yet another nasty shock.

"Get OVER here, Tony!" Pepper Potts barked.

She was kneeling in front of Necrosis where Tony had fallen, gleaming in her crimson and silver Rescue armor. A suit of armor that Tony and Pepper had agreed to retire some time ago. A suit of armor that was much like Tony's, but instead of being equipped with weapons, Pepper's was built for rescue missions. And that technology was currently forming a dazzling repulsor shield that redirected Necrosis's green, flaming laser right back at the deadly robot itself.

The laser was boring a steaming hole into Necrosis's right shoulder, which Pepper—who, Tony was impressed to see was much quicker to figure out the best plan of attack—was trying to redirect into the cut in its hull. Necrosis was backing up as Pepper pressed on, and it was seemingly unable to stop producing the laser.

Tony flew behind Necrosis and grabbed its leg, turning its body so that the laser cut a line across its chest. The flames roared around them.

"Necrosis is pulling back!" F.R.I.D.A.Y. said. "It is no longer attempting to breach our system."

"That's 'cause we have it on the ropes," Tony said.

"We?" Pepper yelled incredulously.

"I'm picking up a pattern," F.R.I.D.A.Y. said. "Every time Necrosis descends into the flames, it only stays there for a short moment. It seems that the fire renders it unable to defend itself and breach other machinery's networks."

"Its own fire slows it down, then?" Tony said. "Let's roast it then. I—"

"With the main power source destroyed, we are operating on reserves," F.R.I.D.A.Y. said. "We will go black in five minutes if we continue expending power at this rate . . . if Necrosis doesn't grab the wheel from me again before we power down."

"Let's worry about now first, huh?" Tony said, giving Necrosis another jerk to the side.

Necrosis used Tony's momentum, though, and moved *with* him. The laser that Pepper was reflecting back at Necrosis shot past the robot and off into the distance of the lab. Now, no longer being seared by its own energy, Necrosis's visor went black, cutting the laser off.

Tony kicked off of Necrosis and joined Pepper's side as she held out her gauntlets at Necrosis, ready for round two.

"I can't believe you're here," Tony said.

"You're welcome—"

"I can't believe you're here. Wearing that," Tony said, cutting her off.

"You're welcome for saving your life," Pepper continued.

"I would've been here quicker, but this thing is a snail compared to you and Rhodey. Not cool."

"Oh, God. Rhodey!" Tony said, his voice falling to a horrified whisper. Necrosis stepped between Tony and the flames where Rhodey was trapped, blocking their way.

"He who reigns . . . over the stars . . . is unconcerned with the likes of you. If you don't burn here, you will surely . . . burn with the rest . . ." Necrosis boomed, staring down at Tony and Pepper. The damage to its hull was visible, but much more minimal than Tony had thought. Beyond the bizarre cut in its hull, there was now a light scratch across the width of its upper chestplate from its own laser. But it was no more than a graze. Tony had been briefly concerned that the damage could've harmed the Ghost if he really was in there, but he knew that the villain could go intangible with a mere thought.

"He who reigns?" Tony snapped. "Cut the vague robot crap. If there's a big bad pulling the strings, tell me, does he have the stones to look me in the eye and tell me exactly how unconcerned he is?"

Necrosis, its visor dark, stared at Tony for a tense moment. Tony braced himself for another attack, knowing that his armor—what remained of it, anyway—would be unable to take another direct hit.

But Necrosis, instead, took off with shocking speed, becoming intangible as it disappeared through the ceiling.

"Should we follow it?" Pepper asked, but Tony, too, was already flying away—and not toward the enemy. Tony barreled into the thick of the fire, screaming Rhodey's name.

There was no answer. Just the mounting roar of the flames.

Tony stormed through the fire, holding his armored arms over his chest to keep his skin from burning. Everything was green, and even through the HUD, his vision was bleary, shimmering from the incredible heat. At any moment, Tony expected to hear F.R.I.D.A.Y.'s voice chime in with a warning, telling him to get out of the raging alien fire before it turned him into a steaming pot of gumbo in his suit, but there was no way that he was leaving this building without Rhodey.

He kicked aside a warped metal table and found Rhodey, face down on the floor like a broken action figure, his lower half submerged in the dazzling flames. No longer caring about what happened to himself, Tony reached for Rhodey and pulled his friend out of the fire.

Vicious heat blasted at Tony's unprotected chest as he turned Rhodey over in his arms, terrified to look at what had happened to Rhodey's face. He had been unmasked in the flames for who knew how long.

Rhodey, his face bruised and bloodied but otherwise unscathed, looked back at Tony through watery, unfocused eyes.

"*Are we . . .*" Rhodey said, his voice pained, "*. . . really just going to hang out in the fire?*"

"Yeah," Tony said, his voice thick. He held Rhodey, looking away from his friend as he blasted off, leaving the blazing green flames behind. He cleared his throat, hoping his voice didn't betray his emotion when he spoke. "Was that not fun? I had fun."

Holding Rhodey close to him, Tony signaled for Pepper to follow him. She blasted up into the air with a smooth, almost soundless takeoff, trailing behind Tony as he shot up through the ceiling onto the upper level. They paused there, hovering over the ruined floor.

"Elevator's a no go," Tony said, holding his free hand up to the ceiling. He hit it with a repulsor beam until the hole he'd made when Nefaria threw him out of the building became big enough for the three of them to get through. They did the same on the next floor, which had now been completely vacated, and then hurried out of the building and into the forest.

Rhodey stumbled away from Tony, holding up his hands. "I'm good, I'm good," he said, wheezing. "Just let me get my footing."

"Besides the obvious devastation and destruction, what happened back there?" Pepper asked.

Rhodey turned to look at her, squinting. "No way. Is that Pepper in there?"

"Do you know anybody else who pilots the Rescue armor?" Pepper asked.

"Give him a break, he was just on fire," Tony said. "And, hey, know what? I'm still catching up to this, too. When did this start being a thing again?"

Pepper raised her face mask and stared at Tony intensely, her green eyes shining. "I wanted to, Tony. Do you need any more than that?"

Tony nodded. "Kind of, yeah!"

Pepper shook her head. "Let me tell you something, Tony. You charge into anything and everything as if there is no one in the world who cares if you live or die. If I hadn't had been there moments ago, both of you would, in fact, be . . ." Pepper exhaled sharply, turning away from them. "I made a choice. It was the right one."

"Let the record show that I am completely on board with that," Rhodey said. "I'm feeling lucky to still have . . . you know, a *face* at this point in time, so I guess I owe you both some gratitude."

"You're welcome," Pepper said.

"Save the gratitude for later," Tony said, looking toward the sky. "Where's Nefaria?"

"Last I saw him, he was sucker punching me and getting the hell out of Dodge," Rhodey said.

"Not good," Tony said. "Whatever he was planning on using Necrosis for, and however the Ghost factors into it, something tells me that he didn't intend for it to set his hiding place on fire. Necrosis is out there now, using Ghosttech, and he's not playing by anyone else's games. If we could only know what Nefaria had planned . . ."

"Looks like everyone is gone," Rhodey said, gesturing to the facility. "They couldn't have gotten too far. We could search the woods and find them."

"Sounds like a plan," Tony said, preparing to blast off into the night. Pepper grabbed his shoulder, stopping him.

"And *if* you found Nefaria, or his men, would any of them tell you what he was doing?" Pepper asked. "I don't think so. We're not going to make any headway pacing around the woods. And going after the entire Maggia with your armors in this state is ridiculous."

"She's got a point," Rhodey said.

"Thank you, Rhodey," Pepper said. "Here's what we're doing. We're going back to the workshop. Tony, you're going to work on repairs for yourself and Rhodey. I'll contact S.H.I.E.L.D. and get them down here before the fire spreads. Maybe *they* can find Nefaria and his crew and ask some questions. Are we clear?"

Tony stared at Pepper for a long moment. "I just had the strangest feeling."

"What is that?" she said, a note of exasperation in her voice.

"You reminded me of someone," Tony said.

"If you say yourself, I'm going to judge you," Pepper said. "For multiple reasons."

"Nope. Definitely not myself," Tony said. "Captain America. And I'm entirely not sure how I feel about that. Part of me is smitten, and the other part of me is shuddering."

"Well, then. Fall in line, soldier," Pepper said, shooting off into the air. Rhodey followed after her with Tony bringing up the rear. He looked back over his shoulder as the green flames blasted out of the windows. The horrific vision fell away as they ascended, becoming nothing but a glinting emerald in a sea of black.

CHAPTER NINE

The Universe Is Listening

Necrosis hovered hundreds of yards over the forest, watching Iron Man, War Machine, and Rescue blast off back in the direction of New York City, like three shooting stars. Even farther below, it could see Nefaria's men scrambling through the darkness of the woods, racing to get away from the burning wreckage of their home.

The people of this world fascinated Necrosis. It had learned much about humanity from the creature known as the Ghost, a being wholly unlike the rest of mankind. The Ghost's technology connected his mind to the various networks that humanity had set up around the world, and now that Necrosis had claimed the Ghost's power as its own, all of those intricate systems that the Ghost had hacked into were in Necrosis's grasp.

It wasn't enough.

This world was nothing like Necrosis remembered. It had arrived long ago, at a time when the world was quiet, to observe humanity and judge their behavior as either worthy of existence or annihilation. But now, the quiet was gone. There was always the distant sound of war, of screams, of murder—that was what Necrosis had been sent to amend, and it could hear the ceaseless beat of violence from thousands of miles away before it even arrived. Violence is never a quiet act. It echoes through worlds, through universes.

And the universe was listening.

Necrosis never got to complete its mission, as its ill-fated landing sent it into the idle state that it had been in until its fateful meeting with the Ghost in the S.H.I.E.L.D. laboratory. When that strange creature, his suit buzzing with thousands of independent networks, drew near Necrosis and woke it from its long slumber, it was like nothing the dormant robot had ever experienced. It was no longer listening to the world's violence.

It was surrounded by it.

Murder, hatred, grief, greed, and wickedness zipped around the world through the invisible threads that bound humanity together. All of that viciousness was a constant now, screaming as it shot from network to network, from person to person, constantly. Communication devices, computers, tools, vehicles . . . and weapons. All of them were linked, even though no one on the planet could see the wires that strung them together. To Necrosis, their connections were golden, vibrant, and dripping with blood.

The world that Necrosis had been sent to judge had grown dark.

Now, using the Ghost-tech, Necrosis was reborn yet again. Without the Ghost's power, the various networks that connected the people of this world were totally foreign to Necrosis. In time, it would adapt and no longer need the Ghost-tech, but it currently worked for the deadly robot as a key. Now, the interlaced web of technology was within Necrosis's grasp; it was the most powerful weapon that had been created by humanity. One of so many, but uniquely deadly.

With the Ghost trapped inside of Necrosis, unwillingly feeding the robot his own power, Necrosis could work its way into so many of these networks from afar . . . but there was a distant whisper among the cacophony that fascinated Necrosis.

Necrosis could crash the world's internet or shut down the power in America's major cities with little trouble. It could spy on anyone in the world with a smart device that was powered on. It could direct traffic to collide, it could crash the stock market, and it could deplete every bank account in the world in an instant. But Necrosis was not an agent of chaos. Necrosis was an executioner, tasked with enacting a swift punishment.

Something about that distant whisper, Necrosis expected, would be useful.

"Show me..." Necrosis said, looking down at its scratched core, behind which was the Ghost, the man who would be the key to Necrosis's mission. "Show me what S.H.I.E.L.D. is protecting..."

Maria Hill was having a bad day.

This was no surprise. Any day that she was forced to make a house call—or, in this case, Bahamian-resort call—to Tony Stark usually meant that things weren't going altogether well for her. In the case of this particular day, though, a hostile sentient weapon had blown up her laboratory, set a good part of the building ablaze, and escaped S.H.I.E.L.D. custody—all under her watch. Having to explain all of that to the president of the United States in a way that still somehow maintained the illusion that she had control of the matter was bad enough on its own, but what came next was worse.

Now, Maria Hill had to somehow *actually* gain control over the situation.

She had deployed teams of her best agents to hunt down Necrosis, and was currently in a Helicarrier headed toward New Jersey with her unit, following up on a call from Pepper Potts telling her that Necrosis had destroyed a Maggia stronghold in the Garden State.

Agent Keith Parks, who was running point under her

command, had jokingly said, "If this Necrosis thing is going to take out our enemies for us, maybe we should just let it do its thing."

Hill couldn't bring herself to laugh, though, when they landed by the burning structure. A local fire unit was already en route to stop the flames from spreading into the surrounding woods, but as the sun rose over the burning building, all Hill could think about was how empty Necrosis had looked before they began to tinker with it. It had been no more sentient than a car. Idle, unfeeling, hollow. Now, it was out in the world, destroying and killing completely off the grid.

"When will we learn to leave well enough alone?" Maria asked, staring off into the woods.

Parks shrugged and spat on the ground. "If we left everything alone, where would we be, you know? This stuff happens. We'll find the item and we'll turn it into scrap metal."

"That was a rhetorical question," Hill said, walking away from him as her cell phone buzzed in her pocket. Plugging her ear with a finger, she spoke into the phone. "Hill here. I'm in the middle of nowhere, New Jersey. Signal is a nightmare, so make it quick."

Maria Hill listened to the hurried voice on the other end, her eyes widening. Parks approached her and asked what was going on, but Hill held up a hand, silencing him. She listened to the report in quiet disbelief.

When the man on the other end was done speaking, Hill choked out her response. "I'm on it. Do what you can there. We obviously can't let this . . . this just *can't* happen. Hill out."

Parks narrowed his eyes. "Who was that?"

"That," Hill said, "was the Pentagon. Someone has hacked into S.H.I.E.L.D.'s restricted military servers. Everyone on our end is doing what they can to keep them out, but they're attempting to access control of missile deployment."

"What do we do?" Parks asked.

Hill gritted her teeth, breathing in deeply and then exhaling. She wanted to scream. She wanted to punch the ground until her knuckles bled. But instead, she stood tall and addressed Parks.

"We're going to do exactly what you said," she replied. "We're going to turn that thing to scrap metal. Now go on. Get those men moving. We need as much information as possible, and we need it now."

Parks clapped his hands together and turned to the rest of the team. "All right, folks, listen up! Within these woods, an entire building's worth of criminals are hiding. They couldn't have made it very far. I want you to flush them all out and bring them back here. We need as much information on what happened here as we can get as quickly as we can get it, and then we have to move out. We have no time to waste on this. Go!"

As the agents ran into the woods, Maria Hill looked toward the sky. The sun rose in the distance, dazzling and orange.

Maria Hill's day had just gotten a lot worse.

CHAPTER TEN

Less Alone

Tony wasn't looking at Pepper while she spoke to him, a habit that he was well aware drove her insane.

They had returned safely to Stark Tower, where Tony had programmed F.R.I.D.A.Y. to run automatic repairs on the Iron Man and War Machine suits after stitching up Tony's arm and injecting him with enough painkillers to keep him moving at 100 percent. Once he was patched up, Tony began dismantling Pepper's Rescue armor himself while Rhodey went on a supply run to Brooklyn to make a pick up from Tony's "guy."

"Your guy?" Rhodey had asked. "Should I even ask?"

"You know," Tony had said, "some people have a guy for, what, cheap tickets to Broadway shows, discount Uber rides? I have a nerdy chemist guy. A supply guy. Just do yourself a favor and don't ask any questions when you get there. Ask a question, he gets excited, he starts talking. We don't have time for talking. I'm talking too much now. Stop listening to me. Go!"

Mercifully, Rhodey had the grace to not ask why Tony needed powdered iron oxide, magnesium, and aluminum powder. Tony didn't want to have to explain that one until the plan was already set in motion.

He also didn't want to have the conversation he was currently having with Pepper, but as evidenced by the way his day was going and the amount of Bahamian sun he was most definitely not soaking up at the moment, Tony didn't always get what he wanted.

"I swear, Tony Stark, if you are sabotaging my suit, we are going to have a big problem," Pepper said as Tony twisted the right gauntlet off of Rescue. "Can you please tell me what you're doing?"

Tony frowned. "I . . . I'm thinking about what you said back on the beach earlier today. Today? Yesterday. I guess it was yesterday at this point. I haven't slept in a very long while."

"You're not answering my question."

"You said—and forgive me, paraphrasing here. You said that you didn't want anything special. You know, you didn't want a whole resort rented out just for you. You wanted to be just someone else on the beach in a sea of faces, just—just a regular person, you said." He popped off the other gauntlet and placed the pair on a tray held in front of him by F.R.I.D.A.Y.'s extendable claws. The claws retracted, pulling the gauntlets away. "Pepper Potts: regular person."

"Yeah," Pepper said, her brow creased. "I said that."

Tony turned to her, flashing a smile. "Liar."

He followed F.R.I.D.A.Y.'s mechanical claws, which were transporting Rescue's gauntlets to the far end of his workshop, where a recent, out-of-use model of the Iron Man armor was laid out like a patient waiting for an operation. Tony absentmindedly wiggled his fingers as he approached it.

"What are you talking about?" Pepper asked.

"Do you know," Tony said, beginning to examine the armor, "what I thought when I started to build the first Iron Man suit? Not the—not the *first* one, not the one I built to save my life. That one did the trick. I walked out of a situation I should've never been able to walk out of . . . and then I went home and built myself another suit. My first *real* suit. Do you know what I was thinking when I finished building it?"

Pepper waited for his reply.

Tony smiled, turning the repulsor in the Iron Man suit's gauntlet to the right. It dislodged from the suit with a satisfying pop. Chucking it from hand to hand, Tony said, "I looked at that first suit—and, I mean, seriously, by my current standard, it looked like something out of one of my dad's sci-fi movies. Bulky, heavy. *So* heavy back then. But I looked at it and I thought . . . *God, this is going to be so fun.*"

He took one of Rescue's gauntlets and brought it over to the table. F.R.I.D.A.Y., programmed to be aware of his next move before he made it, was extending the diamond saw blade.

"Are you saying that's what I think?" Pepper asked. "That Rescue is fun for me?"

"Maybe," Tony said. "Or, or, or . . . or maybe you don't think that. Maybe you've convinced yourself that you're doing this to help me, to pull me back from the edge of obsession, to stop me from going into something crazy—'certifiable'—alone. Maybe. Or maybe you *don't* want to be the normal person, like everyone else, just another person tanning on the beach. Just another exceptionally stunning ginger beauty of a woman tanning on the beach."

"Tony . . ."

"Maybe you know that normal is a story we tell each other so we feel less alone," Tony said, sparks flying up as he cut into Rescue's gauntlet. There wasn't much work to do. He had designed the suit with the thought that maybe one day he would make the changes he was currently making. That was both the advantage and burden to being a futurist—watching the hard times you prepared for in the past becoming the present. "I don't know, Pep. But what I do know is this. The Rescue suit . . . it isn't fit for combat. You walked into something today that could've—should've—killed you."

Pepper stared at Tony, but when she spoke, her tone was much softer than it had been a moment before. "I appreciate your concern, Tony. Seriously. But Rhodey was just *on fire*. And you were . . . I don't even want to say. So I'm sorry that I don't have any patience for your patronizing—"

"Huh!" Tony said. "I thought that was going in a 'thank you for caring, it's heartwarming' direction. Totally misread that."

"Thank you for caring," Pepper said, smirking. "It's heartwarming. And yet still patronizing. I can handle myself, Tony."

"I know," he said. "You're right. Which is why . . ." He twisted the repulsor into the new port on Rescue's gauntlet. Turning it over in his hands, he gave it a satisfied nod before lobbing it across the room, toward Pepper. Confused, she caught it.

"What did you do?" she asked.

"Try it on," he said, turning away from her again to unscrew the other repulsor on the older Iron Man model. "See how it feels. Hey, F.R.I.D.A.Y., pull out a target. Do you have any more of those ones with the Melter on them?"

"One Melter target, coming right up."

"Excellent," Tony said. "Screw that guy."

Pepper slipped her hand into the gauntlet, narrowing her eyes. "Tony . . ."

"The original Rescue armor," Tony said, looking up with a smile as a metal plate, emblazoned with the Melter's sneering face descended from the ceiling, "was designed to live up to its namesake. Rescue missions. Defensive repulsor power. I thought I knew what you wanted, then—maybe I was right. You always told me you didn't want to be a weapon. Of course you didn't. So the suit was an answer to that. But it was an incomplete answer."

Pepper raised her arm and aimed the repulsor on her gauntlet's palm at the target.

"So here's my new answer. My amended answer. Rescue is not a weapon any more than a fire hose is a weapon. You turn that sucker on a person, and yeah, it's going to do some damage. But if you turn it toward what it's meant for—a *fire*—and it does what it's meant to do . . ." Tony said. "Because Pepper? You're not normal. You're exceptional. You came to me when I needed you, out of thin air, and you saved the day. You're a hero. If you want to be by my side in this—and, let me tell you, joining me against Necrosis is about as far from normal as it gets—then we're doing this together."

Pepper thrust her hand forward and a blinding blast of repulsor energy shot from her gauntlet. Tony and Pepper both watched with satisfaction as the target flew across the workshop, clattering against the wall. It fell to the ground, a steaming hole where the Melter's face had been emblazoned.

"You got him right in his ridiculous helmet," Tony said. "I love it."

Pepper sat next to Tony, watching as he put the repulsor in the other gauntlet. In the background, F.R.I.D.A.Y.'s mechanical claws were fitting a brand new metallic mask onto the War Machine armor, quietly clicking and whizzing as the gears of the lab worked on all of Tony's various projects at once.

"Thank you," Pepper said, putting a hand on Tony's shoulder as he worked.

Tony turned to look her in the eyes, and for a moment, they sat there together, smiling. Needing to fill the silence, Tony raised his eyebrows and squeezed Pepper's hand. "Look at this. Actual bonding. This isn't *that* much different from the Bahamas, is it?"

"Oh, it's very different."

"Yeah?"

"Couldn't be more different."

"It could be a little bit more different."

"Really couldn't."

The modifications on Rescue and the repairs on War Machine were complete by the time Rhodey got back. Tony was performing the final fixes to the chestplate he would add to his Iron Man suit, but he had also removed the right arm, which was set off to the side.

Rhodey put the supplies down in front of Tony, breathing out an exasperated sigh.

"Any sightings of the unfriendliest robot?" Tony asked.

"Not sure if you got a good look at it in the club. It's tall, dark, and murderous. Sort of a walking-garbage-can thing going on?"

"No Necrosis sightings, no," Rhodey said, leaning on Tony's desk. "Maybe I would've seen it if I hadn't spent half an hour trying to escape your buddy."

"Did I say buddy?" Tony said. "He's my *guy*. We have a strict client-to-guy relationship. I told you not to mention any inside baseball to him, though. If you show your geek card, he unloads."

"I didn't," Rhodey said. "I showed him the list, he started going off. He said it seems as if we're making thermite; I told him that I *know* we're making thermite, and then he was off."

"See, you should've played dumb," Tony said. "Give him a slack-jawed type face, right? Say something like '*Thermite, that's, like, a cream for getting rid of a really bad rash, isn't it?*' That's how you shut him up. He'll give you this look like he can't believe what you just said, mumble something, and then walk off. It's great. Very fun. Also, you're onto the thermite thing, huh?"

"This isn't my first rodeo, Tony."

"Rhodey's Rodeo," Tony said. "If you ever write an auto-bio, that has to be the title. *Rhodey's Rodeo: The Art of War Machine.* And hey, do me a favor. When Pepper comes back, how about you don't mention the word 'thermite'? Thanks."

"Where is she?"

"She's upstairs," Tony said. "She's in communication with a few of our drones, watching the live footage. Keeping an eye out for Necrosis."

"And why are we keeping the thermite thing from her?" Rhodey asked. "It's the best idea you've come up with so far."

"Right, well . . ." Tony said. "See, if I tell Pepper that I'm installing a thermite bomb in my suit, she's going to ask questions. Any guesses on the first question?"

"Going to go with, 'Isn't that dangerous?'"

"Bingo," Tony said, going through the contents of the bag Rhodey had placed in front of him. They were all set to cook up some thermite. "And, as you know, I won't lie to Pepper. So, in this hypothetical conversation, I hit her with a 'Yes, Pepper, completely dangerous. If Necrosis grabs my arm and squeezes before I get a good shot at it, I'm going to light up like an M-80.'"

"Fun," Rhodey said. "So this is a sane plan."

"Totally sane," Tony said. "Because if I *do* get a good shot at it, we already know the one thing that slows it down: heat. If lighting it up with a repulsor ray won't do it, I'm willing to bet that a thermite bomb placed directly on that cut in its hull might be our best bet at doing some real damage. We just have to make sure Necrosis doesn't—"

"Grab you," Rhodey cut in. "Like it has every time you two have gone head to head."

"Ever the optimist," Tony said. "You know, next time I fix your mask, I'm going to make it hideous. I think I'll even have a pair of honest-to-God googly eyes put on it. That would really strike some fear in the heart of your enemies. If you see a man with a pair of googly eyes, you know there's nothing he holds sacred."

Rhodey laughed and shook his head. But his smile left as quickly as it came. He stared at the War Machine armor, which waited for him across the room. "This is a big one, isn't it?"

Tony nodded. "I'm thinking it is."

"If you hadn't found me when you did . . ."

"Nah," Tony said, waving him off. "You would've charged into the proverbial alien hellfire for me, too. I'm just glad you're . . ." Tony bit his bottom lip, and then forced out a laugh. "Let's make some thermite, yeah?"

"Thermite it is," Rhodey said, and the two of them started to prepare. "You know Pepper's gonna find out."

"Absolutely," Tony said. "But why *not* delay the inevitable?"

When Tony answered his phone and heard Maria Hill's voice sharp with panic, he knew that their situation had just gotten worse. By Tony's estimation, there was no one on this planet more levelheaded and fearless than Maria Hill, with the possible exceptions of Pepper Potts and Steve Rogers—

Captain America himself—so hearing Hill's voice break with fear as she said his name made Tony's heart skip a beat.

"Maria," Tony said, not even noticing that he'd used her first name. He spoke slowly, trying to remain calm as Hill spoke on the other end. "What's going on?"

"We're racing to figure this out on our end, Stark, but we're—we're coming up completely blank," she said, breathless. "Our military servers are being hacked, and our defenses are falling one after the other. I'm being told that within ten minutes, Necrosis will have full access to our military database. That is not only government files, Tony, that is access to missile launch codes. We are on the precipice of an international disaster here, and I'm begging you . . ."

"F.R.I.D.A.Y.!" Tony shouted across the room. "Double down on locating Necrosis, now."

F.R.I.D.A.Y.'s voice spoke through the speaker system in the workshop, coming from all sides of the room. "All of our drones have already been deployed. We—"

"Pick up the speed by ten," Tony snapped, cutting her off. "I need it on sight, now. And set up a firewall over S.H.I.E.L.D.'s network. If we can do to Necrosis what Nefaria's place did to *us*, we should be able to slow it down."

"This thing can breach anything," Hill said. "We have a team of our best working on protections. A firewall isn't going to do it."

"I know," Tony said. "It's temporary. Because I promise

you, we are going to find Necrosis and we are going to stop it. But I'm going to ask you again. One more time. And this is not me asking for government secrets so I can hold them over your head. This is me trying to save as many people as quickly as I can, and I think you're on board with me there. I need you to tell me, Maria, where did you find Necrosis? You sent me all of the files I asked for except *that*, which tells me that's something major, something key. And why are you still, to this very moment, avoiding specifics? Please, let me help you here. It's *me*."

"I found Necrosis!" Pepper came running into the workshop, holding up her smartphone. "F.R.I.D.A.Y., get that footage up."

Pepper flicked her phone, casting an image onto F.R.I.D.A.Y.'s holographic projector in the middle of the workshop. Tony's eyes widened as he saw footage cycling through the various news stations that showed Necrosis appearing from thin air over the Empire State Building. It was looking skyward, casting a thick beam of concentrated green flames into the sky, which was darkening as if a sudden storm was approaching.

"Oh God," Rhodey said.

"It just showed up," Pepper said. "This is live. Not ten blocks from here, Tony."

Tony gritted his teeth, talking into the phone. "We've got a lock on Necrosis, Hill. We're about to take the fight to it.

Send me everything you have on it—everything. Where you found it, why you were looking for it there. Everything. And I swear to you, on everything I love, I will not stop until *it* stops. You hear me?"

Hill said, "I hear you. Hill out."

"Yeah, me out, too," Tony said, shoving his phone into his pocket. "Rhodey, we good on the arm?"

"We're good," Rhodey said.

The gauntlet and forearm armor shot off the table and clamped onto Tony's outstretched arm as he walked toward Pepper.

"Suit up," he said. "Necrosis is already playing out its endgame. We're stopping it. Now."

"What *is* its endgame?" Pepper asked.

"Whatever it is," Tony said, the rest of the Iron Man suit assembling around him as he walked toward the door, "I'm not going to let it happen in my backyard."

CHAPTER ELEVEN

Where They Found It

Necrosis hovered above the New York City skyline, so dark that its colossal form looked like negative space cut from the sky. Green flames flowed from its eye and into the atmosphere above, forming a rolling, tumultuous cloud of blazing energy that collected high above even the tallest building, sending waves of fierce heat down at the citizens below. People had gotten out of their cars in the middle of the street to look up at the fearsome robot that floated over them, unsure if what they were looking at was a spectacle or a real threat.

Within Necrosis, trapped in its innards as if he had been swallowed whole, the Ghost remained paralyzed. While he still couldn't act, his mind was slowly adapting to Necrosis's control, and the Ghost found that he was, once again, aware. He couldn't act against Necrosis, nor could he even move a muscle—but he was alive, and conscious. He could feel himself being used as a tool to Necrosis's end. The Ghost-tech within his battlesuit, enhanced to a level he could've never accomplished without Necrosis's otherworldly power, was worming its way through S.H.I.E.L.D.'s most powerful firewalls, nearing its goal. The Ghost knew what Necrosis was doing.

In mere moments, Necrosis would be able to set off the most powerful missiles in existence. The Ghost felt resistance blocking his tech from both S.H.I.E.L.D. itself and a third party, but it wouldn't be long before those protections were obliterated. Just like the Ghost had dismantled Necrosis's network, Necrosis would use the Ghost's technology to do the same to S.H.I.E.L.D. The only difference was that, unlike Necrosis, S.H.I.E.L.D. wouldn't be able to bounce back from this. The attacks would happen at once, unleashing a level of nuclear devastation unlike any the world had ever seen, effectively decimating the population and physically destabilizing the world. The Ghost wished that was all he knew of Necrosis's plan, but his mind had bonded with Necrosis's own system. He could see the full scope of what it intended to do . . . and he could see what had sent it to Earth.

Necrosis's "memories" of its creator were so terrifying they threatened to shred the Ghost's sanity. All he could do was block the thought from his mind and focus on the more *immediate* dread.

The plan was devastatingly simple. Necrosis was collecting its power, and, moments after the nuclear missiles hit their targets, would then launch the entire cloud of energy into the city in the form of a concentrated ball of flaming death. The energy would burrow into the Earth's core, obliterating one of the biggest cities in the world and causing more destruction in one blow than any single nuclear device. Then, Necrosis would move to Los Angeles to do the same; then Tokyo, São Paulo, Mexico City, and so on. And while Necrosis gathered its energy in each city, S.H.I.E.L.D.'s weapons would destroy the rest of the world with brutal efficiency. Not a single scrap of humanity would remain—no buildings, no record that humans had ever existed. The world would be wiped clean for whatever would rise from the destruction.

The Ghost would almost admire the plan if he weren't strapped in for the ride—a helpless accomplice in the apocalypse.

It was then that the Ghost saw—through Necrosis's eyes—what looked, for a moment, like three shooting stars. They came into focus with great speed, and the Ghost would have laughed if he were able. Iron Man, War Machine, and Rescue cut through the poison-green sky, hurtling toward Necrosis with dazzling speed.

For the first time in his life, the Ghost was relieved to see Tony Stark.

Rescue curved out to the left, War Machine veered right, and Iron Man hurtled directly toward Necrosis.

Necrosis turned to look at Tony, cutting off the green stream of flames it was shooting into the sky. The swirling cloud of alien energy crackled with incredible power above them, radiating heat that Tony could feel even through his suit. It expanded through the sky and then contracted, its movement looking disturbingly like a heartbeat. All that Tony could discern about the energy was that it was getting brighter and hotter by the second, which was enough to tell him that it was trouble.

Right when he would've collided with Necrosis, already lunging to meet him with outstretched claws, Tony abruptly changed course, diving below Necrosis—which, according to plan, flew right into the path of War Machine's missile. The missile exploded on impact, knocking Necrosis down a few yards, but leaving its resilient armor unscathed.

Tony flashed Rhodey a thumbs up as they zipped past each other in the sky. Rhodey prepared another missile as Pepper flew above Necrosis, holding both hands out in front of her. She bent her arms and thrust her palms forward, unleashing twin repulsor beams at its head. Tony flew closer to Necrosis, zeroing in on its damaged core as he prepared to launch the thermite bomb.

Necrosis phased out of tangibility just as Pepper's attacks would've hit. It flew toward her and, with a shimmer of bright energy flowing up its armor, became corporeal once again as it launched a series of energy blasts at Pepper from its visor, putting her on the defensive. The blasts came one after the other in small bursts, like automatic gunfire, chasing Pepper as she looped through the sky, avoiding them with the grace of a dancer—until one clipped her right gauntlet, which exploded in a blinding burst of repulsor energy.

"Pep!" Tony cried out, speeding toward her.

"I'm fine!" she shouted, using her other hand to send another repulsor beam at Necrosis, just as Rhodey unleashed another missile.

Necrosis went momentarily intangible, shimmering like a reflection in rippling water as the missile phased through him. It continued shooting downward, rocketing toward the civilians below.

"Tony, shoot it down!" Rhodey cried as Necrosis sped toward him.

Tony was already on it, sending a repulsor blast toward the missile. It exploded in midair as Tony and Pepper flew toward Necrosis, side by side.

"Pep, Rhodey. Necrosis is only phasing when it's on the defensive," Tony said. "I need a good shot at that chestplate. I hate to ask, but can you make sure it's firing at you?"

"You bet," Pepper said, turning upward. Tony, relieved that she didn't question his plan, circled around Necrosis, which was fending off blast after blast from Rhodey while charging up its visor with what would be a vicious blast of emerald fire.

"All right," Tony said, holding the arm equipped with the thermite bomb out in front of him, waiting for his shot. "Let's see just how much heat you can take."

When Necrosis went intangible, War Machine's missiles phasing through its body and down toward the city, the Ghost felt something familiar. It was as if something was calling his name in the darkness, but it wasn't quite a voice, nor a physical feeling. It was deeper than that.

The Ghost closed his eyes and reached out as best he could toward the familiar buzz, and he began to feel something that was akin to déjà vu. As Necrosis phased back into its physical state to send a deadly beam toward Rescue, the feeling was gone, cut off.

What is that? the Ghost wondered silently, his nerves aching to reach out. *Who are you?*

Necrosis phased again as Pepper sent a huge, shimmering repulsor blast at it, and the feeling was back, stronger than ever. The Ghost closed his eyes and reached through the darkness, the same darkness into which he had originally descended to commune with Necrosis, and he saw a shape forming before him. It blinked away every time Necrosis became physical, but got stronger and clearer as Necrosis phased more and more often.

The Ghost was looking at all of the interwoven networks

that Necrosis was working its way toward, a glowing, tangled mess of information, of numbers, of names, of secrets . . . networks that the Ghost had been in before. As he reached further and further, bolstered by the feeling of far-off familiarity, the Ghost realized that he was regaining strength each time Necrosis dipped into the power of his Ghost-tech.

Necrosis was mere moments away from breaking through S.H.I.E.L.D.'s final defenses, a system the Ghost himself was more than familiar with.

The Ghost reached out for the web and felt it reaching toward him as well.

Yes, he thought, still silenced by Necrosis but no longer paralyzed. *You recognize me, don't you?*

The glowing information before him that he knew was S.H.I.E.L.D.'s last defense began to shimmer, trembling. It was about to break.

The Ghost grasped the system, aware that as soon as he acted against Necrosis—if he truly could act against it— that would be *it*. He wouldn't be able to escape before it destroyed him from within, obliterating his tech with a mere thought and sending him falling from higher than the highest building in New York City.

But the Ghost wasn't going to out like that. No, if he had to go out, and it was looking as if he did . . . he was planning on taking Necrosis with him.

The Ghost grasped the information and pulled it closer

to him. *Give me everything you've got,* he said as S.H.I.E.L.D.'s network bonded with his own Ghost-tech, sending every form of malware that S.H.I.E.L.D. had ever encountered into his own system and, by extension, Necrosis. Before the Ghost tapped into the system itself, the malware had no way into Necrosis's network, but with the Ghost as a willing conduit, the viruses traveled through the Ghost's system and into Necrosis, which began to shake violently.

The Ghost knew it would kill him, but he couldn't help but laugh. At least he was the one who got to pull the trigger.

Necrosis must have been aware of Tony's plan to keep it on the offensive. As Pepper and Rhodey tried to bait it into attacking them, it continually flitted in and out of tangibility, making the robot impossible to grab. Then, suddenly, as Necrosis was phasing through the top of a skyscraper, attempting to make Pepper hit the building instead of it, Necrosis suddenly came back to its corporeal form, destroying the top of the building.

"You see that?" Rhodey said, diving toward a visibly rattled Necrosis.

"What was that?" Pepper asked.

Tony, circling the area as he waited for them to set up his shot, followed them while they bounded toward Necrosis, who was shaking off the rubble from its armor. "F.R.I.D.A.Y., what's happening with Necrosis?"

"Its system is faltering," F.R.I.D.A.Y. said. "It's fighting off a seemingly endless number of viruses that are attacking its operating system on all fronts."

Necrosis unleashed a stream of flames, and Rhodey flew toward it. He curved sharply to the side to avoid the stream by what had to be an inch, at most, and grabbed Necrosis's left claw. Necrosis raised its right claw to come down on Rhodey, but Pepper clamped onto it from behind. The two of them flew backward, spreading Necrosis's arms widely.

At that moment, Necrosis began to shake violently.

"Whoa!" Rhodey shouted.

"Is this thing going to explode?" Pepper cried out.

"Hold it still!" Tony said, stretching out his right arm. "We've got one shot here."

"Do it, now!" Rhodey said.

A panel in Iron Man's armor opened up, revealing the thermite missile, which extended from the forearm panel. The missile launched out of the armor with an ear-splitting whistle and penetrated Necrosis's core before the shaking robot could even attempt to dodge it.

Tony couldn't help but grin as webbing—an equal parts helpful and disgusting gift from Peter Parker, New York's friendly neighborhood Spider-Man, who had given Tony some of his own organic webbing to use as an adhesive in his armor repairs—shot out from the missile, gluing it to Necrosis's damaged hull.

"Let go!" Tony shouted to Pepper and Rhodey. "Get clear of Necrosis, now!"

Rhodey and Pepper dove away from Necrosis, which fumbled with its arms, still vibrating horribly from whatever malfunction the mysterious malware was causing. As the thermite, its temperature soaring to above five thousand degrees Fahrenheit, shot out of the missile in an awesome shower of sparks and flames, Necrosis fumbled to remove the missile with its free claw, which began to bubble and sizzle.

"Tony!" Pepper called as the three of them careened through the air away from Necrosis. "What was that?"

"Thermite. Sorry, I should've told you," Tony said. "You would've stopped me. I could've lost an arm. Or a body. But hey—looks like it's working!"

"Oh my God. Is that . . ." Pepper pulled away from Tony and looked toward Necrosis as the fountain of sparks and flames continued to shoot off of its chestplate in midair. But something else was happening. At first glance, it looked to Tony as if one of Necrosis's arms was falling off. Pepper saw what was really happening though. "There's a person in there!"

A limp, human form slipped out of Necrosis's flaming body. Pepper took off toward the falling man, swooping low, moving faster than she had ever flown in her Rescue suit before. The ground rushed toward her as she sped down, her arms outstretched, the world a blur of silver and green and blue.

At the last moment, Pepper latched onto the falling man, holding him tight against her armor with her one functioning gauntlet. She kicked off, right as they would've hit the ground, and flew away from a group of awed onlookers, taking the unconscious man to a nearby building.

She set the Ghost down on the rooftop, causing a group of pigeons to scatter. Tony landed next to her, menacing in his silence. He looked down at the crumpled man, who twitched on the ground, his bulbous helmet lolling about on his shoulders. His battlesuit was scorched, and the hosing that extended from the power pack on the back of his suit into his neck and helmet was charred, sending off noxious plumes of smoke. But even with the damage, he was alive, his chest rising and falling with wheezing breaths.

"That's the Ghost," Tony said. "I knew it. I knew this waste of life was involved. He is the reason Necrosis has been able to go intangible. It's his tech that allowed Necrosis to hack into S.H.I.E.L.D.'s servers."

"Is their connection broken, then?" Pepper asked.

Tony aimed his hand at the Ghost's head, readying a repulsor beam. "One way to find out."

"It . . . wasn't me," the Ghost croaked, holding up a clawed glove. "It . . . I tried to control it. Couldn't . . . it's too strong."

"Was too strong," Tony said. He gestured to the sky, where Necrosis was still hovering but kept dropping lower and lower, consumed in flames and sparks. Rhodey was floating across from it, all of his missiles trained on the robot, watching to make sure it didn't free fall to the ground while it was still flaming.

"That won't kill Necrosis," the Ghost said. "I still feel it. It burrowed into my mind . . . used my tech to override all of my programming. It was trying to—"

"Yeah, I know what it was trying to do," Tony said. "You and Nefaria were in on this together, huh? Trying to repurpose the big, bad alien robot for yourselves?"

"Yeah. Just like you and S.H.I.E.L.D. were," the Ghost snapped. But then, as he looked out at the horrific green cloud in the sky, he sighed deeply and turned to Tony. "You have to destroy it."

"Thanks for the tip," Tony said with a sneer. "I'd be a lot closer if you hadn't given the damn thing your phasing powers."

"I tried taking it down myself. I cut it off from my powers, hit it with a bunch of viruses . . . but that didn't stop it, and neither will this. Whatever you did, you saved me . . . but I'm getting the impression that wasn't your goal. It can't complete the hack without me, but look up there." He gestured to the collection of violent green energy that thrashed in the sky, somehow dark and bright at the same time. "When it gets back up—and trust me, it will get back up—it's going to send all of that right into the Earth's core. It'll do it at every major city until . . ." The Ghost brought his hands together and then extended his hands in an explosive gesture.

Tony bent down to the Ghost and grabbed him by the neck. "This is on you. Necrosis was idle until you came into S.H.I.E.L.D. and woke it up. Everything that happens from now, everyone that gets hurt, everyone that died at Nefaria's . . . that is on you, and I will make sure you pay for it."

"*Henh*. You do that," the Ghost said. "You know what can do the trick . . . it's *heat*."

"I know, heat slows it down," Tony said. "You're not telling me anything we didn't already figure it out."

The Ghost shook his head. "It doesn't just slow it down. I watched Nefaria's people cut it open with concentrated, prolonged heat. You just hit it with—what was that, thermite? That was good, but you need to go bigger. I mean, you know where they found it, right?"

Just as Tony opened his mouth to answer, F.R.I.D.A.Y. was good enough to pull up the file from Maria Hill on his HUD—after all of his insistence to get Hill to spill the beans, he had been so preoccupied with the battle that had hadn't seen it yet. Tony scanned through it as the Ghost stared at him through his helmet. Tony's breath caught in his chest as his eyes swept over the words. Not only did the new report, now with the previously classified information included, detail where Necrosis had been found, but also why Maria Hill had refused to let Tony know about it until it escalated into a doomsday situation.

"Yeah," Tony said, his lips set in a grim frown. "Yeah, I know where they found it."

"Then you know what to do," the Ghost said. "Question is, how are you gonna get it to make that trip?"

Tony was already looking through a map on his HUD. "I don't think I'll have to."

"What is he talking about?" Pepper asked.

"Tony!" Rhodey called, his voice chiming in over their linked armors. "This is going south, fast."

Tony and Pepper looked up to see that Necrosis was now spinning violently in the air, ascending once again as Rhodey flew after it. When it came to a stop, thick smoke rising off of it, Tony zeroed in on Necrosis and scanned it with his HUD. Its core was completely decimated now, a mess of melted armor and open, sparking wire . . . but it still seemed to be functioning perfectly, its green eyes flashing even more brightly than before.

"Pepper, stay here and make sure this idiot doesn't escape," Tony said, shoving the Ghost away as he walked to the edge of the building. He looked up and locked his sights on Necrosis, which was once again shooting its green flames into the sky, completely unmoved by the onslaught of missiles that Rhodey was sending its way. The missiles exploded on impact, each of them hitting the target now that Necrosis could no longer exploit the Ghost's phasing power, but it didn't matter. It didn't even bother to fend them off.

"That is impossible. What you hit it with would've taken out *anything*," Pepper said, her voice hushed. "It's . . . it's invincible, isn't it?"

Tony looked at Necrosis through his HUD, the words from Maria Hill's report on its discovery lining his vision. From Tony's point of view, the report looked like bars of a jail cell, with Necrosis trapped behind it.

"No," Tony said, clenching his fists. "No, it's really not."

CHAPTER TWELVE

Something Big

As victorious cheers erupted around her, Maria Hill felt hot tears spill down her cheeks.

She and her team, along with the few low-ranking members of the Maggia that they'd captured in the woods, were on the S.H.I.E.L.D. Helicarrier headed for an emergency meeting at the Pentagon, where she would have laid out a worst-possible-scenario plan to the president of the United States. The truth was that, if those missiles had been deployed, no plan of action that she could offer would have been enough to compensate for the devastation that would have happened on her watch.

Now, she didn't have to walk into that building and stifle her anger long enough to give an empty speech about rebuilding, about gaining trust, about showing the world—what was left of it—who the real enemy was. She had just received the call that the Ghost-tech that had been disabling their firewalls in an attempt to access S.H.I.E.L.D.'s nukes had suddenly disappeared, as if it had never been there to begin with. The danger was still clear and present, and S.H.I.E.L.D. agents were already en route to attempt to put an end to Necrosis. For all Hill knew, their victory was momentary.

Best-case scenario, Hill was aware that even if she led her people to victory against Necrosis, which she promised herself she would, she'd still have a lot to answer for in the coming days. Such a breach would have surely resulted in, at best, the leak of classified information and knowledge of S.H.I.E.L.D.'s weapons spreading to the people, the press, and even their enemies. At worst . . . Hill couldn't even think of the "at worst."

"Director Hill?"

Agent Parks stood at the passageway leading to the forward observation room, holding a gently glowing tablet. He cleared his throat. "I have an updated report to send to the Pentagon, pending your approval, Director Hill."

Hill nodded. "I'll be right there. Thank you, Agent Parks. Let everyone know that we're heading to New York, now. Agent Leonard McKelvey's unit will beat us to the city, but I want to be *there* to end Necrosis myself. Make sure we have units on the ground, and that civilian evacuation protocols have been put in place. This is going to get messy, so we need a wide perimeter here. Iron Man, War Machine, and—I'm told *Rescue*—are already at the scene, so we'll need weapons in air and in place on the ground. Am I understood?"

"I'm on it, director." Parks bowed his head slightly and turned around, heading back into the observation room.

Since becoming director of S.H.I.E.L.D.—and, in fact, even when she was an entry-level agent—Maria Hill had seen threats that everyone had overlooked and counted out rise up to strike back when no one was looking. No, she knew that this fight was far from over. But another thing that she had learned in her line of work was that one of the most important things someone can do is allow herself a moment to celebrate victories, no matter how small. And this one, though still incomplete, was decidedly *not* small.

Now, it was her job to ensure that the next victory would be complete.

Another great wave of heat blasted down toward New York City as Necrosis continued to shoot its laser into the atmosphere, amassing a growing pool of swirling fire in the sky. Tony Stark, his gleaming Iron Man armor reflecting the alien energy above, stood on the rooftop next to Pepper and the fallen, defeated Ghost, watching as War Machine launched ineffective attack after ineffective attack at the demonic robot.

"Tony," Pepper said, keeping her single functioning gauntlet pointed at the Ghost, ready to subdue him with a concussive blast of power if he made a false move. "What are you thinking?"

"Hill just uploaded Necrosis's classified files to F.R.I.D.A.Y.," Tony said, readying himself to launch into the sky. "I know where they found it."

"Tell me you have a plan!" Pepper called after Tony as he blasted off toward Necrosis.

"I do," Tony shouted over his shoulder. "I'm going to put it *back*. But first, we have to take care of the atomic pea soup floating over the city."

Speeding toward Necrosis, which was now pushing itself lower to get farther from the intense heat of the cloud of fire that floated above the New York City skyline, Tony's mind started racing. He knew what he had to do to shut Necrosis down, but he needed to weaken it more first. *And* he needed to get rid of that deadly mass of alien flames that threatened to obliterate his city.

"Rhodey!" Tony shouted, shooting out a concentrated repulsor beam at Necrosis's open core. Rhodey, who was valiantly firing another series of missiles into the robot, saw what Tony was doing and flew over to meet him in the sky. Rhodey launched a red repulsor beam alongside of Tony's, hitting the same spot in Necrosis's marred armor. Tony grinned within his helmet, appreciative of how quickly his friend caught on.

Necrosis began to vibrate as they pumped repulsor energy into its armor, which was starting to whine as the beam cut through it. Despite that, Necrosis was focusing all of its power on completing the flaming cloud above, and was allowing their beams to eat through its armor, which unnerved Tony to no end.

"Unless . . ." Tony said aloud.

"Unless? Unless what?" Rhodey said, putting another burst of strength into his beam. "Why are you talking in the *I have a dangerous plan* voice? You know I'm not a fan of the *I have a dangerous plan* voice."

"F.R.I.D.A.Y.!" Tony commanded. "That special suit I have you working on. The Melter-proof one! How quickly could you get it here?"

"The heat-resistant model isn't yet equipped for drone surveillance, sir," F.R.I.D.A.Y. replied. "I had to momentarily stall production on it to render the repairs needed to the current Iron Man and War Machine models."

"Not talking about a drone," Tony said through gritted teeth, giving the repulsor another wave of power. "How fast can you get it here and onto my body?"

Necrosis's visor shot a final stream of green flames into the cloud. The energy zipped away from its visor, which turned black as it turned to look down at Iron Man and War Machine, the massive wall of green flames above it beginning to spin in the sky above, completely blotting out the sky behind it.

"I've deployed the suit," F.R.I.D.A.Y. said. "Fifty-five seconds. I must warn you, sir, while the suit is resilient, it isn't yet complete. There will be no, as you'd requested, *swimming in volcanoes*. I would need ten more minutes before it would be up to par with what you wrote in your blueprint."

"I'm not even sure if we have the fifty-five seconds," Tony said, still firing his intense repulsor beam and looking up at Necrosis in horror as it lifted its claws into the sky, which began to glow with sparkling green energy that matched the terrible cloud of flames.

"That's new," Rhodey said, the panic in his voice matching Tony's.

"Yeah," Tony said. "Not good."

"This world," Necrosis boomed, its voice setting off a series of wailing car alarms below, "has eaten away . . . at its own core. You, the people who inhabit . . . this planet . . . are a disease. Necrosis will not . . . allow it . . . to spread!"

Necrosis swung its arms down, and the massive cloud of thrashing emerald flames followed the thrust of its claws. The gigantic cloud of energy funneled into a brilliant, concentrated ball of vicious power the size of a small car. It sped downward like a comet, toward the city, shining with blinding light and radiating waves of heat that made Tony's eyes sting within his armor. The only things standing between the terrified people below and the blazing ball of alien energy were Iron Man and War Machine.

* * *

"So," the Ghost said, leaning back on his elbows and looking up at Pepper. "Who are you, then? The Iron Maiden?"

"Yeah, right," Pepper said, glaring down at him. "I think Tony would like that a little too much."

"*Henh*," the Ghost laughed, but the sound came off too warbly to sound genuine. Since accepting what he'd thought was his certain death when he allowed the viruses to flood his and Necrosis's systems, he hadn't been able to stop trembling. And Pepper knew it. "Are you really going to point that thing at me until he gets back?"

Pepper stood silently over the Ghost for a moment, the glowing repulsor in her gauntlet reflecting back at her from his shining helmet. "You want to talk?" Pepper said, wishing she could glance over her shoulder to see what was happening between Tony and Necrosis. The heat was mounting, and she could hear the flames roaring above them, louder than ever. But she knew that taking her eye off of the Ghost for even a fraction of a moment would be a move that she'd regret. "Fine. Let's talk. What was in this for you?"

"Same that's in it for you," the Ghost said. "Same that's in it for Tony and—uh, that other guy up there. Battle Bot, or whatever his name is."

"I find it hard to believe that."

The Ghost raised one of his hands, and Pepper held the repulsor out at him, which hummed as she prepared to launch an attack.

"Not being sneaky," the Ghost said, raising both hands skyward. "I'm just saying. These suits . . ." He touched his wrist, moving it around in his grip. He clicked his power inhibitor on then off, on then off. "They're not weapons. Everyone calls them that, you know? That's why Nefaria hired me. To get him a weapon. *Become* a weapon for him, basically. But if we get it right—and trust me, Iron Maiden, I'm man enough to admit that I decidedly did *not* get this one right—then we aren't weapons, are we? We're . . . we're *more,* more than the rest of them, more than ourselves."

"How inspiring," Pepper said flatly. "A psycho with a superiority complex. I'm very surprised."

"Are you talking about Stark?" the Ghost asked. His held his hands in the air, as if he was being held at gunpoint.

Pepper glared at him, not answering. She watched his finger tremble in the air.

"Well," the Ghost said. "Thanks for this little talk. My system should be rebooting just about . . . *now*. So see ya!"

As soon as the Ghost slammed his clawed glove down on the rooftop, Pepper launched a repulsor blast at him—but it was too late. The rooftop on which she stood became intangible as the Ghost touched it, and Pepper fell right through before she even realized what had happened. The interior of the building blurred by her as she phased through floor after floor until she finally hit solid ground with a loud *clang* that vibrated through her body.

Her heart racing, Pepper leapt to her feet and looked from side to side. It was an office building that, mercifully, seemed to be empty. Empty and dark. On her left, an elevator. On her right, a window.

She knew which one she had time to use.

Making a mental note to contact the owner to pay for the property damage at a later date, Pepper took off through the window, the glass shattering around her as she shot out of the building like a bullet. She curved around to the top of the building, ready to light up the rooftop with her repulsors, but when she got a clear view of where she had been standing, her heart sank in her chest.

The Ghost was gone.

It had been his trembling fingers. By the time Pepper realized he was making a move and not just shaking, he'd already touched the building. It was too late.

"I'm sorry," Pepper said, speaking to Tony and Rhodey through her suit. "The Ghost slipped away. I could try to track him, but . . ."

Pepper looked up at the sky, and what she saw hit her like a swift punch to the gut. Necrosis was pointing its claw down, sending what appeared to be an emerald comet down at Tony and Rhodey, who were being forced down toward the city, attempting to hold it off with a weakening repulsor ray.

"Here I come, Tony," Pepper said, and sped off in the

direction of Iron Man, hoping desperately that she could make good on her code name.

"Fifty-five seconds *has* to have passed!" Tony yelled, throwing more power into the repulsor beam shooting into the green inferno. It was absorbed right into Necrosis's devastating attack, which barreled down toward Tony and the city below, unhindered by their attempts to slow it down.

"Twenty seconds remaining," F.R.I.D.A.Y. said.

Tony shot a glance to his side as he and the concentrated ball of flames descended on New York City. Rhodey was right by his side, shooting repulsor blasts into the flames.

"Rhodey, go!" Tony cried.

"What? Are you crazy?"

"Yes!" Tony barked back. "Go and make sure Pepper doesn't try to get close. I'm . . . I'm going to do something big, okay?"

Without another word, Rhodey sped off, and Tony was alone, facing the blazing green ball of energy.

"F.R.I.D.A.Y.," he commanded breathlessly. "Take the suit off of me!"

"Sir, you are free-falling toward Manhattan in the face of a deadly blaze of extraterrestrial flames, and the new model isn't yet—"

"Take the suit off of me now and encase that—deadly blaze of whatever you just said in it. You got it?"

"Sir—"

"Now!"

Tony felt his suit pull off of him, piece by piece. Both the whipping wind and the unbearable heat of Necrosis's fire hit Tony at once as he free-fell toward the city below.

The Iron Man suit wrapped around the blazing green comet before him, but it was still descending toward Tony too quickly. For a horrible moment, Tony was certain that his plan wouldn't work. His suit would fail to contain the attack and he would be incinerated before he could even hit the ground below.

Then, before Tony's bleary eyes, the Iron Man suit expanded and re-formed into a sphere of gleaming scarlet and gold, catching the flames in midair and bringing the attack to a sudden stop.

"Now!" Tony screamed. "Send it back at that ugly—"

Seconds before he would've hit the ground, Tony was snatched out of the air by what must have looked to the panicked civilians below like a UFO careening through the sky too quickly for them to make sense of its appearance. Tony felt his new heat-resistant Iron Man suit, cool to the touch after his skin had been singed from the horrific flames, form around him, encasing his body in its smooth metal.

"Longest fifty-five seconds of my life!" Tony said as his new helmet clamped shut. "Now . . . let's see some fireworks."

He looked skyward as his last Iron Man suit, which was breaking down before his eyes, sped toward a baffled Necrosis with the robot's own fireball inside of it. Necrosis, realizing what was happening at the last minute, unleashed a stream of its blazing energy into the sphere, but it was too late. The suit, containing the full force of Necrosis's apocalyptic attack, was already too close to Necrosis to stop. The robot attempted to dodge it at the last moment, but the flaming ball of its own energy slammed into Necrosis. It exploded on impact, lighting up the sky with a flash of hot, green light, shattering glass in the buildings below as the shockwave of sound rippled through the city, and setting off every car alarm within a mile of the impact.

"Rhodey, you hear me?" Tony, shielding his field of vision as the energy dissipated from the sky. He couldn't see Necrosis yet.

"We're here!" Rhodey called, zooming over to him. Pepper was at his side. "You scared the hell out of us, Tony."

"What kind of plan was that?" Pepper shouted, looking as if she was ready to strike Tony out of the air herself.

"We have to find it, now. If there's anything left, that's just *part* of the plan," Tony said, beckoning for them to follow him. There, Tony saw Necrosis, or what was left of it, slowly floating toward the ground like a balloon losing its helium, leaving a trail of acrid, black smoke in its wake. "F.R.I.D.A.Y., speak to me. Do we have anything coming off of Necrosis?"

"Indeed we do. It's giving off a stronger signal than ever—which means its protections are down. Every part of the robot was dealt intense damage, which leads me to believe that there was no central source of its power. No hard drive. I believe that its programming is perhaps engrained in the substance out of which it had been constructed."

"Meaning we have to hit it *harder*," Tony said.

"Meaning just that," F.R.I.D.A.Y. replied.

"Good thing we planned for that," Tony said. The three of them shot down through the sky, toward Necrosis, which now appeared as a warped, melting mess of what it once was.

"We did?" Pepper asked. "We planned for *what*?"

"I have to destroy every little bit of it," Tony said. "And I know how to do it."

"Slow down a sec, man. What are we doing?" Rhodey said, preparing his rocket launcher and repulsors as they got closer to the falling Necrosis.

"Follow my lead. Grab it and don't let go—no matter what. Be prepared to launch into absolute top speed at my command," Tony said. "We're taking Necrosis for a ride."

War Machine charged ahead of them and snatched Necrosis's arm, grabbing it out of the air right before it would've crashed into a skyscraper. Rescue clamped onto

Necrosis's head, which had drooped down to the center of its melting chest and wrapped her arm with the functioning gauntlet around its misshapen, twisted neck. Finally, Iron Man flew into Necrosis's core and grabbed its innards, the thick wires sparking and smoking from the damage caused by its own attack.

"Follow my lead!" Tony commanded, blasting off toward the coordinates on his HUD. "And Pepper, watch out for its eyes!"

The three of them flew, Necrosis in tow, leaving the Manhattan skyline with a sonic boom that echoed throughout the city.

Thick smoke continued to flow out of Necrosis, crowding Tony's vision, but F.R.I.D.A.Y. was running the suit on autopilot, closing in on their location. Tony felt Necrosis's wiring suddenly grow taut, as if the deadly robot had regained consciousness.

"You . . . will not win," Necrosis's voice boomed from inside its core.

"Yeah, well," Tony said, pushing Necrosis even harder as he felt it start to mount resistance against the three of them. "Neither will you, buddy."

Their target came into sight. They sped through the open skies of Pennsylvania, high above swaths of green hills and twisting roads, approaching the closest open mineshaft that F.R.I.D.A.Y. had been able to find.

Necrosis had been discovered in a North Korean mine-shaft, Tony knew now. And S.H.I.E.L.D. most certainly did *not* have clearance to be there . . . which explained Maria Hill's hesitance to broaden the circle of those who knew about Necrosis's true origin. Tony wasn't sure who had buried the thing deep in the earth, but hoped that taking it back down there would shut it down or destroy it. He needed a mine or a volcano, somewhere that had enough heat to do what needed to be done, and the best F.R.I.D.A.Y. could come up with was this Pennsylvanian mineshaft that had been sealed after a failed experiment with geothermal energy.

"F.R.I.D.A.Y.!" Tony shouted as they pushed Necrosis. "What am I in for here?"

"The mineshaft was closed after an eruption of lava," F.R.I.D.A.Y. replied. "I must caution you once again that the suit is *not* prepared for f—"

"So you're saying it's still cooking below," Tony said. "Good."

"Tony, what are you thinking?" Pepper asked, a hitch in her voice.

"Just keep pushing!" he said, driving Necrosis downward.

If he couldn't destroy Necrosis, he could at least take it down to a place like the one that had shut it down previously. He believed that there was some sort of protection built within Necrosis's system that prevented physical harm from coming to it. That same protection must have rendered it idle, which would explain why the robot had still been intact when it was discovered in the depths of the mineshaft, but why sudden and concentrated heat damaged its hull by hitting it before it was able to initiate its protection.

If a thermite bomb or the brunt of its own apocalyptic energy couldn't destroy Necrosis, the mineshaft was Tony's best—and only—bet. He just had to hope he'd damaged the robot beyond its capacity to shift into the invulnerable, comatose state that had allowed it to withstand the last time it was exposed to this level of heat.

"I've got a grip on Necrosis now!" Tony shouted. "Pepper, get down to that mineshaft and make sure no one is around. Rhodey, once Pep gives you the clear, I want you to light it up! Everything you've got!"

"Why?" Pepper asked. "What are we doing?"

"*I'm* doing it," Tony shot back. "Go! Trust me!"

Pepper broke off from them and dove toward the ground. Tony pressed harder on Necrosis, whose defenses were growing. It was starting to push back against Tony as it regained its power, but Tony had enough momentum that, if he didn't have to stop to defend himself from an assault, he could at the very least get Necrosis into that mine.

Pepper's voice filled both Tony and Rhodey's HUDs as they descended on the mineshaft. "We're clear!"

"You're up, Rhodey!" Tony called.

"You . . . will . . . die!" Necrosis boomed, shooting out a sputtering ray of green flames. It was no good. Tony was too close for it to hit him, so the attack shot off into the distance, dissipating in the sky.

Rhodey pulled away and aimed all of the many weapons built into his suit downward. A brutal onslaught of firepower rained down on the sealed mineshaft, which exploded in a cloud of flames and smoke. Tony headed right for it, holding on to Necrosis with all of his power.

Tony heard Pepper cry his name as he and Necrosis shot, full speed, into the flaming mineshaft, cement and earth crumbling around them as they disappeared into the ground. As Necrosis's power mounted and the cords that made up its innards began to wrap around the Iron Man suit, squeezing him in his armor, Tony closed his eyes and pushed onward, down into the darkness.

CHAPTER THIRTEEN

Reaching Beyond

Rhodey landed on the burning ground next to Pepper, who was preparing to charge into the flaming mineshaft after Tony and Necrosis. He grabbed her arm, stopping her at the precipice of the depthless gorge.

"Hold on," Rhodey said, holding tight. "You can't do that, Pepper."

Pepper turned to him, her mask snapping open to reveal her wide, terrified eyes. "Rhodey, we can't let him go in there with that thing alone. The temperature alone—"

"Our suits can't take it," Rhodey said. "That suit F.R.I.D.A.Y. sent was something special, I think."

"You think?" Pepper shouted, ripping her arm from Rhodey's grasp. "Tony Stark just dove into an *exploding mineshaft* with an alien sent here to destroy the world, and you *think* he has some kind of . . . what, impenetrable suit?"

Rhodey stood across from Pepper, noxious smoke rising from the gaping hole in the ground behind them. Ripped caution tape was strewn all over the ground, curling from the intense heat in the air.

"I think—sorry, I *know* we have to trust him on this one," Rhodey said. "He said he has a plan. You know better than anyone—better than me—that when it comes down to it, Tony Stark is ten steps ahead. Now, the second he calls for me, you can bet I'm going down there. But until then, until Tony says otherwise, if this is his plan? I trust it."

Pepper took off her helmet and threw it to the ground in frustration. She stared down at the ruined mineshaft, the flames from Rhodey's missiles roaring from deep within. It sounded like the ocean. Beyond the flames, all she could see was pitch-black darkness. No dazzling blue repulsor blasts fending off streams of green energy, nothing. Just *nothing*.

Pepper closed her eyes and breathed out. "I trust him, too," she said, hoping that hearing herself say it aloud would help her believe that Tony would emerge from that nothingness, already imagining what clever, annoying, wonderful thing he would have to say. It didn't make her feel better, though. The hardest part of knowing and loving Tony Stark wasn't when he was infuriating her. It wasn't even when he disappointed her. The hardest part was when Tony was there, right next to her, with her—and then, the next moment, gone. So many of Tony's enemies, and even some of his allies, knew Tony as a self-aggrandizing, ambitious-to-a-fault, thrill-seeking narcissist. Pepper knew that Tony would be the first to own up to any of those qualities. The thing was, those who thought that missed the truth of Tony Stark, the thing that Pepper loved the most about him. The same thing that scared her the most about him.

Tony Stark was a hero, through and through. He might have looked at his first fully equipped Iron Man suit and mused at how *fun* it would be, but Pepper knew that story was just another instance of Tony skirting around what he really meant, and what he really felt. Iron Man didn't exist because Tony loved taking joyrides across the country. Iron Man existed as an answer to something that Tony thought was missing from the world, something that prevented it from being the best world it could be.

That was the truth of Tony Stark. He was Iron Man because he needed to be, for himself and for the world. And that meant he would do anything to follow through on the promise he made to the world the moment he first put on that suit.

He would protect the world until the end of the line.

Suddenly, a third voice chimed in over their HUDs, making both of them jump. "Stark? Colonel Rhodes? This is Maria Hill, come in."

"Hill, this is Rhodes," Rhodey said.

"I'm looking at a New York City skyline that is suddenly missing our runaway robot," Hill said. "Did you and Stark just save the day and forget to tell me?"

Pepper and Rhodey shared a look.

"I'll get back to you on that one," Rhodey said.

"I'm sending you our coordinates now," Pepper said. "Get your people here, Maria."

Silence followed, and they took that as Maria Hill agreeing to meet them at their current location, though both of them desperately hoped they wouldn't need S.H.I.E.L.D.'s help. Rhodey gazed down into the scorching mineshaft and said exactly what was on Pepper's mind.

"Stark, if this is a suicide mission, I'm going to kill you myself."

Tony, holding tight onto the thick, alien wiring, which shot out hot, green sparks and writhed wildly, like snakes in his grip, smashed Necrosis through another layer of concrete. They were far, far down in the depths of the mineshaft, and the temperature was mounting with every level of ground they broke through. Besides the immense natural heat, Rhodey's missiles had done exactly what Tony had hoped— they'd broken the seal of the mineshaft, but they'd also turned the entire pit into a blazing furnace. Tony's current standard Iron Man model would have failed to withstand the temperature at this point, but his Melter-proof, heat-resistant suit was doing the trick. The suit's repulsors were weaker than his normal ones, and it felt heavy in a way that he hadn't felt with his armor in a long while, but he wasn't being liquefied within it—yet—so the additional weight was the least of his many worries.

Necrosis continued to fruitlessly blast out progressively weaker streams of green fire, and its attacks did nothing but add to the crippling heat that surrounded them. Tony knew, though, that if he let up on Necrosis, even for a second, that it would regain the strength to rip free of Tony and free itself from the inferno they were creating deep in the ground.

"You cannot stay in here much longer, sir," F.R.I.D.A.Y. said, as Tony's HUD flashed red with warnings, displaying the rapidly increasing temperature next to an approximation of how long it would take him to get back up to the safety of the surface. Those were numbers that Tony didn't like, so he chose—as he did with most things he didn't like—to ignore them. "The suit is incomplete. I urge you to abandon—"

"Nope. Not gonna do it," Tony said, blasting Necrosis down through another blockage. Every time they emerged into an open fall, the temperature shot up mercilessly. He felt a bead of hot sweat drip down his neck. "Not gonna bail. This has to end, right here. Now."

"It . . . won't." Necrosis's words were no longer backed by the frightening, thunderous voice that once boomed from all parts of its machinery at once. The sound that came from the robot was like an old, heavy, creaking door. Whining and pained, barely audible.

Tony took that as a victory.

Heat blasted through his suit, stinging his eyes. He wondered how much longer he had. His HUD had the answer, right there in front of him, so he closed his eyes and pushed harder.

"This . . . is no . . . conquest," Necrosis wheezed as they broke through another blockage. "You will . . . die alone. Here and now."

"Don't think so. If I'm gonna kick it, you're *definitely* coming with me, pal," Tony said, and found that he no longer had to push. Necrosis wasn't resisting. Now, they were freefalling, and there were no more blockages between them and the bottom of the mine. They slammed, together, into sizzling-hot volcanic rock, surrounded by lava that surged around them, shooting up past them from the pressure. If Tony's eyes were open, he would see streams of blinding orange shooting up around them like geysers.

The world around them was on fire.

"There is no death . . . for Necrosis."

"Yeah? I think you might be wrong about that." Tony stood weakly, his knees buckling. Sweat poured down his face and, for one ridiculous second, he had the impulse to remove his helmet. He snickered at himself, shaking his head.

Necrosis, its cords bursting into flames, looked up at Tony, its visor gleaming with the reflection of the lava around them. "I am one of many . . . a single cell of a larger body."

"What does that mean?" Tony said, standing over Necrosis. "Huh?"

"Necrosis is . . . not a single being. Necrosis is a *sentence*. Others like . . . this model . . . will come."

"If you're a sentence, who is the judge? Who sent you?"

"It is no secret . . ." Necrosis groaned. "Necrosis comes in the name . . . of the Celestials."

Tony balked at that, squinting as sweat burned his eyes. "The Celestials?" he repeated.

"The army is endless," Necrosis said. "Extinction will be swift."

Tony hadn't been expecting that. The Celestials were as old as the universe itself, a powerful race of creatures who were referred to as "gods" by people who used such words. Larger than life and above time and space itself, they had certainly interfered with life on other planets before, which had led to them coming into conflict with members of the Avengers, Tony included. However, sending a deathbot down to Earth was a new level of aggression that unnerved Tony beyond words.

If he made it out of this oven, he would have a whole new set of problems to worry about.

Tony looked down at the warped, melting robot. A sparkling wave of green power began to spread over its armor.

Tony was sure that this was the defense mechanism that protected its body, but that shut its system down—and Tony was not ready to end the conversation.

Tony put his gauntlets on Necrosis's helmet and blasted it with a repulsor beam. The shimmering green began to recede.

"Why?" Tony barked. "Why are the Celestials sending you—your army, whatever? What did the Earth do to get in their crosshairs?"

"He who sees . . . saw what this world would become. . . . And it is even worse than he anticipated when sentient life first sprang about . . . on the Earth," Necrosis said as Tony's repulsor beam filled its head, shining through its visor like a jack-o'-lantern. "The people of this world . . . are destroying it. . . . You have created your own weapon to stop them from . . . killing themselves. . . . Who will stop the people of this world . . . like the people of so many others . . . from reaching beyond, into the universe, and destroying that, too? The people of Earth . . . deserve to DIE!"

Necrosis let out a final blast of vicious green energy from its visor, which hit Tony directly in the chest. He felt the armor, weakened by the extreme heat, cracking on his body—and he knew it meant that if he didn't get away from Necrosis at that very moment, his suit would break and leave him vulnerable to the immense heat, which would cook him alive in an instant.

But Tony wasn't moving. Instead, he moved his hands, still blasting out the repulsor beam, onto Necrosis's visor. Just as screaming-hot pain cut through Tony's hand, Necrosis's head filled with green light and then exploded in a blinding flash of green flames and repulsor energy, sending Tony careening away. Tony hit the wall, hard, and slumped down to the ground, searing pain eating away at his hand, which was steaming in his cracked gauntlet.

Tony looked at the melted remains of Necrosis, standing in amazement for a moment. The robot's core melted into the ground, snapping and bubbling like burning soup, and running off in black streams of goo into the lava.

He couldn't believe it. Necrosis had finally been destroyed.

Or *one* Necrosis had.

Tony cursed as his skin begin to burn against his armor. There was nothing quite as sobering as realizing that your entire body is about to be on fire. He bent his knees and shot up, moving as fast as he could, rocketing up through the flaming mineshaft, hoping that the red, flashing numbers on his HUD were wrong.

Behind Tony, the surging streams of lava blasted up toward him, flowing up through the mineshaft.

Horrified, Tony pushed on, closing his eyes. The roar of the lava built like a wave, deafening.

"I'm gonna make it," Tony told himself. "I'm gonna make it, I'm gonna make it, I'm gonna—"

Tony's armor flew off of him, shocking his body with a burst of cold air as he emerged from the mineshaft, as if the ground had spit him out. His Iron Man suit fell on the grass off to the side, which burst into flame as soon as the sizzling-hot surface of the armor touched it. Tony hit the ground hard and looked up at the sky as the world spun above him. He held his hand to his chest, gasping in the fresh, cool air in deep gulps.

"Wha—watch out! Lava!" Tony cried. "Lava!"

"Tony!" Pepper ran over to him, lifting him up to his feet as she hugged him. Her armor was cool against his bare skin, which made him suddenly aware that he was standing on public property in the middle of Pennsylvania, in front of Rhodey and Pepper, in nothing but a pair of burnt underwear.

"Hey, Tony. Do you . . . uh, need to borrow a pair of pants?"

Tony winced. He recognized that voice. And it didn't belong to either of the people he'd come there with.

"Uh, yeah, Cap," he said, wincing, refusing to look at Captain America. "I could go for a pair of pants."

"I don't know," another familiar voice said, dripping with sarcasm. "That's kind of a good look for you."

Upon hearing Black Widow's voice, Tony spun around to see the Avengers gathered before him. Captain America, standing at the front of the group in his red, white, and blue garb, clutching his shield, was flanked by a smirking Black Widow and Thor, who held his hammer, Mjolnir, at the ready even as he let out a mighty laugh. Hawkeye, Spider-Man, and even the Hulk, who had already transformed into his monstrous green form in preparation for battle, were cracking up.

Tony looked back at the open mineshaft. "There's . . . no lava."

Thor peered down into the fiery depths. "It seems to have stopped a good distance below. But the denizens of this good city shall surely want this hellhole covered."

Tony breathed a sigh of relief and shook his head. His legs were trembling violently, his heart racing. It had been a close one indeed.

"You guys are just in time," Tony said, spreading his arms wide and strutting across the battlefield, deciding to stifle the leftover dread and embrace the embarrassment. He was, after all, alive . . . and not currently on fire, which was a pleasant surprise. Compared to how things had looked seconds before, he figured he was doing okay, indecent exposure or not. "I know I'd asked you all to come help me take out Necrosis, but Pepper, Rhodey, and I already have that on lock. World saved, crisis averted. We're all good here. But you know, I *think* I saw someone littering back in Manhattan while we were pounding on Necrosis. Guy just throws a napkin right on the ground. *That* is a job for the Avengers."

Black Widow raised a brow, smiling at Pepper. "He's extra snarky on account of *he's naked.*"

Pepper nodded. "I think you're right."

Tony sighed, looking at the flaming mineshaft. He would have to have a conversation with the Avengers about Necrosis—where it came from, why it was sent, all of that—before they left. But for now, Captain America was right.

The world was saved, and Tony Stark needed a pair of pants.

CHAPTER FOURTEEN

However Temporary

The Ghost floated weightlessly down the long, dark corridor that led to the technological haven he called home. Because of his power to phase out of corporeal form, he no longer needed a physical place to rest. But even though he had left behind so many of the things that made a person human, there was a certain comfort in having a place that was only his. A place to sit, to think—to call his own.

He phased through the wall that led to his den of Ghost-tech, which would perhaps appear to the untrained eye as the poorly designed interior of a spacecraft from a low-budget sci-fi movie from the '50s. In actuality, this strange, underground room was home to the largest and most powerful computer in the world—at least, the most powerful computer that the Ghost knew about. He called it his second brain.

As he entered the room, a strange, buzzing urge rippled through his body, and he felt pain in the depths of his chest. For a horrible moment, he thought that Necrosis had somehow reached back through their connection to take control of his systems once again, but this felt nothing like the oblivion that giving into Necrosis had offered. The strange sensation passed as soon as it came, and the Ghost was momentarily confused as to what had caused it, but then the knowledge of what he'd felt settled in with grim certainty: Necrosis was dead.

Or, rather, destroyed. Something that was never alive to begin with cannot die.

The Ghost stood slightly hunched in his room, grey panels with seemingly endless rows of buttons surrounding him. Rows and rows of hard drives, ports, and screens filled the room, which was bigger than a football stadium by ten- or even twentyfold. In its voluminous space, the Ghost felt utterly alone.

Though Necrosis had used his body and technology against his will, the Ghost experienced something akin to mourning for the alien robot. True, he had wanted Tony Stark to stop it from destroying the world, and he'd passed on the tip about Necrosis's weakness for vengeance, but there was something undeniably tragic about its destruction. In this world, Necrosis had been utterly unique—the only system of its kind to ever journey to this planet. That, the Ghost figured, was something worth mourning. People came in droves. Necrosis was singular. The Ghost knew that there were more of them out there, and for an absurd second, he was fascinated at the idea of the army of Necrosis bots arriving all at once.

This world wouldn't stand a chance.

Just as he was wondering if he should reach out to Tony Stark to warn him of the distant threat, a metal object clinked against the back of the Ghost's helmet. Before he could turn to see what had struck him, he heard a familiar, oily voice.

"What's the matter?" Count Luchino Nefaria said, holding his pistol up to the Ghost's helmet. "Have I interrupted your brooding?"

The Ghost, snickering, turned around. Nefaria stood before him, expressionless, wearing a royal-blue suit fitted to his slender form. His dark eyes were set in a hateful stare, and the Ghost knew right then that his betrayal hadn't gone unnoticed. Nefaria held the gun out in front of him, trained directly between the Ghost's eyes.

"How dramatic," the Ghost said, his tone sour and harsh. "What is this, you came here to tie up loose ends?"

"You murdered countless men in my employ," Nefaria said. "Burned down my home. It follows that I owed you a visit to yours. You must have known I would come for you."

The Ghost sighed bitterly, shaking his head. He agreed silently; he should have expected Nefaria to come after him with questions, but he had been so drained by the whole ordeal that he hadn't even thought of it. If he had, he would've found Nefaria and phased up through the bottom of his bed while he was sleeping, becoming corporeal only once his fist were clenched around the wicked man's heart.

A missed opportunity, that.

"Listen, guy," the Ghost said. "Two things. One . . . I didn't do anything to your people, or your place. Necrosis did. Hijacked my system. Chewed me up, spit me out. Tried to destroy the world while he was at it. Do you not watch the news?"

Nefaria didn't respond. He also didn't lower his gun.

"And two . . . even if it was me—which I know you know it wasn't—what do you think you're going to do with that gun?" the Ghost asked, making himself intangible as he spoke. He held out his incorporeal hands, phasing them through each other. "You can't shoot me. If I wanted to, I could make the entire *floor* intangible before you even pull the trigger. I just did it to Iron . . . I don't know, Iron Woman, Iron Lady, something. It was hilarious."

Nefaria frowned. "You think me so incapable that I would come here and threaten a man with a gun that I wasn't *certain* I could use? My resources are not insubstantial, Ghost. If I wanted a gun that could kill you, I could—I *would*—have such a thing made." He lowered the gun, passing it to his other hand, and then back. "I could also do it with my bare hands. Before you'd be able to move against me, I could crack through that ridiculous dome of yours, just in time to see your expression as you die. But still . . . there is something elegant about a gun. Classic. Maybe that makes me a *thug*. Interesting."

He raised the gun again, smiling.

The Ghost, unsure whether or not to believe Nefaria, stared at the barrel before him. He wondered how it would feel to die. At least Necrosis had someone to mourn his death. No one would grieve if the Ghost were murdered.

"I didn't," the Ghost repeated, "do it."

Nefaria stared at him through narrowed eyes, studying him. "I believe you," he said slowly, but he didn't drop his weapon. "On the other hand, I have had an incredibly frustrating day. Beyond your failure, and the price I've paid for it, you fled as Necrosis destroyed my home. Killed my people. While you stood by doing nothing, Iron Man and War Machine invaded my facility. They humiliated me. They— they put one of my men in a *tree*. He soiled himself. I ask you, Ghost, is that how men treat other men?"

"Well, you're pointing a gun at my head because you've had a crappy day, so I don't really know how to answer that."

Nefaria's eyes lit up, and he let out a barking laugh. The Ghost could hardly contain his sigh of relief when the man across from him tucked the gun into his belt, his chest still rising and falling with laughter.

"Heh . . . hah . . . that's excellent," Nefaria said, shaking his head. "You have a point. Now, tell me. Necrosis. Where is it?"

"Wait, why? You can't possibly want to try again."

"Where . . . *is* . . . it?"

Not wanting to see that gun again, the Ghost told him the truth. "Dead." When Nefaria cast him an inquisitive glance, the Ghost amended his word choice: "Destroyed, I mean. Stark. Have you not seen the news?"

"I don't currently have a *television*, Ghost," Nefaria said. For a moment, the Ghost thought he was going to go for his gun again, but instead he turned around and delivered a sharp kick to the wall. His foot went through the metal as if it was a sheet of tissue paper.

Nefaria cursed loudly, spitting each word out, and the Ghost felt a strange solidarity with the man. Necrosis had been a mindless, uncomplicated killing machine, not unlike a gun . . . but it was as intricate and beautiful to the Ghost as he was sure other people considered works of art to be.

The Ghost considered telling Nefaria what he knew, about the army of Necrosis-bots that was tucked away in the darkness of space, waiting for a signal that, for all the Ghost knew, Necrosis might have sent out before it had been destroyed. While he was trapped within Necrosis, his network tied to the robot's operating system, the Ghost saw flashes of Necrosis's descent to Earth. He didn't know how long ago it was, only that the world had been a very different, and a very quiet place when Necrosis had first landed. The impact of the landing split open the planet, engulfing

Necrosis in immense heat. Before it could even begin its judgment of the planet, it had had to initiate its emergency protection system, a defense that put it into the stasis in which S.H.I.E.L.D. had discovered it. It could have so easily gone differently . . . and if more Necrosis robots did end up coming, as the Ghost was sure they would, the planet Earth would not be so lucky a second time.

If Count Nefaria knew about that, he would stop at nothing until he'd located the army himself. Whereas the Ghost was just glad to be alive at this point, he knew that Nefaria saw Necrosis's escape as a personal failure, one that he could only rectify by completing his original plan, no matter how insane it was.

"Unfortunate," Nefaria said, turning around. He began to walk away. "However, tomorrow is another day. I will come calling on you, Ghost."

The Ghost wondered if he was tempting fate, but decided that he couldn't help himself. He floated after Nefaria, hovering over him. "Why?" the Ghost asked, his raspy voice echoing through the cavernous room. "What are you really trying to do here? Yeah, kill the Avengers, bring corporations down, take over anything that . . . anything that *could* be taken over. But why? What are you trying to do?"

Nefaria held the Ghost's gaze for what seemed like eternity before a wide, wormy grid spread across his face.

"To make the world a better place."

The Ghost hovered in his room, watching as Nefaria disappeared at the end of the long aisle of hard drives, his footsteps echoing throughout the room, loud and sharp, like gunshots.

Tony, now wearing a shirt and a pair of pants he'd bought from the discount store in the town a few miles from the mineshaft, bit into a slice of his favorite pizza in all of Philadelphia. There was something about almost getting broiled in his own suit of armor that made a man ravenously hungry.

Tony sat at the pizzeria's biggest table with Pepper and Rhodey—still in their armor but unmasked—Captain America, Hawkeye, Black Widow, Spider-Man, Bruce Banner (no longer in Hulk-mode, and also sporting a discount–store shirt—his was purple while Tony's was black), and Thor. They were all digging in to their second slices of pizza, except Thor, who had opted for a plate of penne alla vodka.

"Who gets pasta at a pizza place?" Hawkeye said, pointing his thumb at Thor. "This guy thinks he's fancy."

"There are but few mortal delicacies that can live up to the bounty of an Asgardian banquet, but these noodles surpass all other cuisine," Thor proclaimed, wiping orange off of his mouth with his meaty fist. "Banner, pass me a garlic knot. I wish to dunk it in my sauce."

Tony glanced both ways, making sure no one was in earshot. The owner of the shop, a wizened, old man who spoke in grunts and had more hair coming out of his ears than he did on the top of his head, always did right by Tony and cleared the place out when he had to talk shop. Just like he had a supply guy, he had a pizza guy in all of the states that were worth eating pizza in. Besides, he knew Thor would order more food within the hour they were there than the man would normally sell on their busiest Saturday, so it all worked out in the end.

"We might have a bit of an intergalactic problem," Tony said, his voice hushed. "This is definitely a cross-that-bridge-when-we-come-to-it type of situation, but I figured I would let you know. Apparently, Necrosis is one of a—what did he say, endless army? An endless army acting on behalf of the Celestials."

"What beef do they have with Earth?" Cap asked.

Tony bit his bottom lip. "Don't know. Not even sure if it's *true*. According to Hill's file, Necrosis had been sealed up for—who knows, for a *very long time* before they dug it up. And we've butted heads with the Celestials since then, and none of them seemed especially shocked that the Earth was still swinging around the sun. Something's off here."

"Hold on a second," Spider-Man said. "Is no one going to address the fact that Cap just said 'beef'?"

"I was going to let it slide," Black Widow said with a grin, playfully nudging Captain America, who rolled his eyes.

"Are you thinking that Necrosis was trying to throw you off of your game?" Pepper asked. "If it lied about who sent it to purposely send you down the wrong track, that might give the real enemy time to prepare another attack."

"Or," Rhodey said, "for all we know, there are more Celestials out there than we're aware of, right? Universe is a big place."

"Getting bigger by the day," Banner said.

"Captain America said 'beef,'" Spider-Man said. He looked around at the other Avengers, spreading his arms. "What? That's funny!"

"I'm going to look into this," Tony said, finishing off his pizza. "And then, I'm going after Count Nefaria and the Ghost. If they know something, I'll find out."

"Hate those guys," Hawkeye said with a grunt.

"All right," Tony said, wiping his greasy fingers on his new shirt. "Good seeing you all. Thanks again for the massive help. Couldn't have done it without you. Go team, go."

"I finished saving the entire continent of Europe half an hour ago," Black Widow said. "Do you hear me bragging?"

Tony turned to Pepper. "I'm off to check in with Hill . . . but you and I have to have a chat. An important chat. Away from here, away from everyone. Especially these guys. I hear that Bruce Banner has a hell of a temper. Can't be trusted."

"Hulk jokes," Banner said, sighing. "Never gets old with Tony Stark."

Tony squeezed Pepper's shoulder. "I'll have a jet waiting for you when you get back. Take your time here. I think Thor has about ten more pounds of food to order, so there's no rush."

"I could certainly go for a dish of linguine," Thor said brightly.

"A *jet*?" Pepper said, incredulous. "Tony, I'm exhausted. Where could you possibly want me to go?"

Tony winked at her, sliding out of the booth. He clasped hands with Rhodey, and their eyes met. Both men knew the other had almost died that day, and were freshly reminded of how it would feel to lose their best friend. There were no words Tony could force out to deflect how he felt about that. He was grateful.

By the time Tony left the pizzeria, a drone-operated Iron Man suit was landing by the storefront. A group of kids gathered around, taking pictures of it with their camera phones. Tony whistled, motioning for the suit to come toward him.

The group of kids stared in awe as it disassembled into pieces of red and gold metal and snapped in place on Tony's body. As Tony walked past them, the suit forming with every stride, he turned around to face the kids. Now fully armored, Tony called them over.

"You want a *really* cool picture?" Tony asked. "The

Avengers are in there, pigging out on some pizza. Very disgusting. A true show of gluttony. Post that picture, you'll be raking in the likes, big time."

As the kids hurried toward the window of the pizzeria, shoving and arguing over who was going to get to post the picture online first, Tony took off into the sky just as the sun began to set, painting the sky with dazzling pink and orange. Just hours before, the sky above New York City had been blazing with green flames that were meant to destroy everything humanity had built since the beginning of time until today. All of those buildings, all of the people within and around them, all of the life that Tony had vowed to protect.

There was a lot of work ahead, but as Tony rocketed through the warm, radiant sky as day fell to night, he felt his heart swell with pride. It looked like there was a fight to come, but he'd won this one.

Night had fallen by the time Tony Stark arrived at the S.H.I.E.L.D. facility from which Necrosis had first escaped. Repairs were unsurprisingly already well underway, and Tony was sure that, in no time at all, it would look just as boring as ever, as if a killer alien robot hadn't launched the first of its attacks in a plan to destroy the world right within those walls.

"Gotta love S.H.I.E.L.D.," Tony said, striding toward the building.

Maria Hill was already on her way out the door, walking away from the facility with a long coat covering her uniform and a briefcase in her hand. She looked down at the ground as she walked, her short, brown hair hanging over her face, obscuring it from sight—but Tony Stark knew that power walk anywhere.

When she was within earshot, Tony's face mask popped open, and he called out to her. "Leaving so soon, Hill?"

She looked up, her face registering mild surprise. She paused for a moment, as if considering what to do, and then changed direction, heading toward Tony. He strode toward her, meeting her halfway. He'd seen her briefly after emerging from the mineshaft, when she and two teams of S.H.I.E.L.D. agents arrived just in time to turn right back around and leave. Tony had invited Hill to grab pizza with the Avengers, but she had places to be, reports to fill out, and power walks to walk.

She held out a hand, which Tony took, and gave a firm shake to. A strangely formal gesture from two people who had just worked together to save the world.

She chuckled softly, rubbing her hand on her coat. "Cold."

"You say that now. If you shook my hand half an hour ago, I'd be taking you to the hospital with a third-degree burn."

Hill offered him a weak smile before clapping her hands on her side. "Did you need something? I was just heading out. It's been a long . . . well, I would say day, but I haven't been asleep in I think more than *two* of them. If I drink another cup of coffee, I think I'm going to vibrate my way into an alternate reality."

"That's actually possible, I think," Tony said. "Caffeine-induced dimensional travel. Research must be done."

Another half smile passed over her lips. Tony narrowed his eyes, leaning in toward Hill, the concern clear on his face. She averted his gaze.

"Hey," Tony said, his voice soft. "What's up? What's wrong? You just smiled at me, twice."

Hill shook her head, but didn't look him in the eye. "Nothing. Why did you come here? I told you that you didn't have to fill out any reports. My people have it covered."

"That's bull. And I'm here because here is where you are," Tony said. "I wanted to, among other things, tell you that there is bound to be something left of Necrosis deep in that pit. Wires, whatever it's made out of. Not sure if any of it would be useful. I also don't know how you'd get it, but I saw you already have a team working on putting that fire out. I don't think it can regenerate—not after what I saw happen to it. But still. Worth a look. Oh, just be careful. There's lava. Have you ever seen lava in person? Not as exciting as you'd think. Less fun, more existential dread."

"After all that, you think S.H.I.E.L.D. has any interest in attempting to adopt Necrosis's tech?"

"Um. Based on, historically, everything S.H.I.E.L.D. has done, maybe ever? Sure, I do. Also, if you don't go down there and get it, someone will. Maybe Nefaria, maybe the Ghost. Hell, maybe—maybe the Melter. Maybe the Melter will step up and make me rue the day I doubted him and his silly, silly helmet. I figure I'd rather you and your boys tinker around with that tech than any of them."

Maria Hill looked up into Tony's eyes, her expression fraught with emotion. "The devil you know, huh?"

Tony tilted his head to the side, looking at her curiously. "You know, I'm wondering, did I miss something? Did something happen besides the near-doomsday scenario? You're acting decidedly un-Maria Hill-like. What gives?"

"Nothing. Stop."

"No. I'm going to annoy you until you talk. Don't make me be immature. You know I can be immature. I'm just going to talk and talk and talk until you—"

"God. It's amazing. The smartest man in the world is an overgrown eleven-year-old."

"I'll pretend I just heard the compliment there. I can be happy with that. Talk. Spill. What's up?"

"I don't know. I suppose you were right, Stark," Hill said. "This . . . all of this, Necrosis, the missiles, it's all on S.H.I.E.L.D. This is on *me*. Maybe you can joke around the same day that an extraterrestrial enemy, which I ordered to be excavated from the ground, hacks into our system and tries to deploy weapons that would devastate half of the world . . . but that's not me. If I had told you from the beginning where I got it, this would've all been solved sooner."

"You couldn't have known," Tony said. "Though, North Korea? Really? That's a bold move."

"Some information is classified for a reason," Hill said. "We don't want to have any international incidents with North Korea, but we also don't want a hostile government to have something with untold power—like Necrosis—at their disposal."

"And what happened to the North Korean miners that found the thing in the first place?"

"Come on. I'm not Count Nefaria, Tony," Hill said, shaking her head. "Nothing 'happened' to them. You know S.H.I.E.L.D. has psychics in our employ, who–"

"You wiped their minds!" Tony exclaimed. "That is *definitely* something happening to them."

"We removed a specific memory that would've endangered them in their own country. I'll sleep tonight," Hill said. And then, after a pause, she looked at Tony, the defensive edge gone from her voice. "But still . . . I should've trusted you. If I had . . ."

"If, if, if," Tony said. He took Hill by the shoulders, looking her right in the eyes. She darted her gaze away, but he stared her at her unblinkingly until she met his gaze.

"What are you doing?" Hill asked.

"*If* you hadn't dug that thing up, someone else would've. Someone who wouldn't be torturing themselves if it did send off those missiles. *If* that had happened, today would've maybe been a lot worse. *If* you had told me where you got it from the jump, maybe I would've gotten it done faster. Maybe not. But it's still done. You can't think about *if. If* didn't happen. You were doing your job."

"And you cleaned up my mess."

"You were doing," Tony repeated, "your job. Hey, you know, it's funny. Not this conversation. This is unfunny. I'm thinking about—have you ever noticed how, in TV and movies, comics, and all that, scientists are usually the bad guys? Evil scientist doing *evil science?*"

Hill furrowed her brow. "Um. Sure?"

"Scientists make great bad guys," Tony said. He let go of Hill's shoulders and turned around, looking off into the night sky. The cool air washed over his face. "Evil doctors creating monsters. Wicked men in lab coats trying to 'play God.' Even well-meaning smart folks trying to do something good, who end up just . . . just raising hell. It's a trope. Know why?"

Hill waited for him to continue.

"Because people are scared to ask questions," Tony said,

holding up a finger and nodding. "Yep. The unknown is terrifying, right? But the idea of going into the dark and looking the unknown in the face and asking, 'Hey. Unknown. What *are* you?' That's even scarier. And anyone who does that—anyone who dares to ask *why*, dares to ask *how*? That person must be *mad*. But really, the truth is, if we all just left well enough alone, we would—what, we would be driving stone cars we pedal with our feet and naming our kids after rocks. Do you know what I'm saying, Hill?"

Hill looked him in the eye, her troubled gaze softening. "Maybe."

"It's your job to ask *why*," Tony said. He held her stare for a moment before smiling and turning away, his face mask closing as he prepared to take off. "Later, Hill. Ease up on the caffeine. This dimension needs you."

"Hey," Hill called after him. "Stark."

Tony looked over his shoulder, the eye slits of his helmet glowing white in the dark night.

"You really came through today," Hill said. "Saying 'thank you' sounds cheap."

"I don't mind cheap," Tony said. "You should see the shirt I'm wearing under this. I think it's made out of mulch."

Iron Man blasted off into the night, disappearing into the sky until he was just a glint of light among a sea of stars. He had one more place he had to be.

* * *

Tony Stark arrived at the resort in the Bahamas before Pepper Potts that night, and this time he didn't even need F.R.I.D.A.Y. to remind him. He landed on the beach where he had sunbathed with Pepper what seemed like forever ago. In actuality, two entire days hadn't even passed.

That night, Tony knew he would sleep deeply.

He sat down on the beach, which was silent except for a warm, whistling wind. The resort had been kind enough to honor his reservation, accepting no other guests, even though he and Pepper had both left ahead of schedule. As Tony placed his Iron Man helmet in the sand next to him, he said, "Hey, F.R.I.D.A.Y.?"

The helmet lit up, and F.R.I.D.A.Y.'s voice chimed in: "Yes?"

"Remind me to leave a big tip. I'm thinking twice the normal."

"You've got it."

"How long until Pepper's jet arrives?"

F.R.I.D.A.Y. paused, causing Tony to sit up in the sand.

"F.R.I.D.A.Y.?" he asked. "What's the deal? Looking for an ETA here."

"Pepper . . . didn't board her jet, sir."

"Huh? Why not?" Tony asked "There was a jet waiting for her. Who doesn't like a good, old-fashioned ride in a jet? She can't *still* be eating pizza. If Thor is hitting on her, I swear,

I'll kick his Asagardian butt. Wait, hold on—Pepper is okay, right? Is—"

"Look skyward, sir," F.R.I.D.A.Y. said.

"F.R.I.D.A.Y., come on. Don't play coy with me. You're AI. You're supposed to make my life easier." Tony swept his eyes over the sky, baffled. That confusion lasted only for a moment, as what he had initially thought was a plane moving through the dark sky was actually flying much faster than any commercial aircraft, heading right toward him. For a chilling moment, Tony thought Necrosis—or, rather, *a* Necrosis—was descending from the sky, ready to carry out the mysterious Celestial death sentence.

Rescue came into view quickly, creating a wave of cool, clear water as she sped toward Tony on the beach. Tony launched himself into the air to avoid the wave, which crashed onto the sand where he had been standing a moment earlier. Landing in the wet, white sand, Rescue looked up at Tony. Her face mask popped open, revealing Pepper's bright smile.

"Are you just going to float there, or are you going to join me on the beach?" she called up to him, laughing.

Tony lowered himself down to the sand until he was standing right across from Pepper, the starlight playing across her armor. Even in the suit—maybe especially in the suit—she was the most gorgeous woman Tony had ever seen.

"Hi," Tony said. "Are you trying to impress me? Is that what this is?"

"Says the man who rented out an entire resort for a date," Pepper said.

Tony pursed his lips, nodding. "Fair. That's fair. So I'm that transparent, huh? You knew I was coming here?"

"Yep. You kind of are."

"It was supposed to be a surprise," Tony said, brushing a lock of red hair away from Pepper's face. "You know, you get on the jet, you don't know where it's taking you. You land, and then, boom—Bahamas. Surprise."

"You're a smart man, Tony. That doesn't mean you're a subtle man."

"*Also* fair."

"And F.R.I.D.A.Y. confirmed it for me," Pepper said with a mischievous smile.

"That AI has a big, big loyalty issue," Tony said. He looked over his shoulder, yelling toward his discarded helmet. "We're going to talk about this, F.R.I.D.A.Y."

"Enjoy your weekend, sir," F.R.I.D.A.Y. said as the lights on the Iron Man mask dimmed, leaving Tony on the beach with Pepper and the dim, dazzling light from the stars and the moon, which hung high in the sky, a perfect white circle.

Pepper took Tony's hand in her own. "I know this is just tonight . . . I know you'll have to get back to work tomorrow.

Especially with Necrosis, and what you found out. I don't expect . . . I'm just glad we're here. I'm glad we have tonight."

Tony shrugged. "I was planning on extending our stay. I mean, if you don't want . . ."

"You don't have to get back?"

"If an army of killer robots shows up to try to end the world, I'm thinking we'll know about it," Tony said. "Now, if I do extend the reservation, the rest of the nights won't be just us. There will be other people. Kids, even. Screaming kids with floaties on their arms. If we do stay the extra days, we'll just be another couple on the beach. Two normal people. Two normal people who saved the world today."

"There is nothing normal about you, Tony," Pepper said, smiling up at him.

"Likewise," Tony said.

He and Pepper sat on the beach and, for the whole night, they didn't talk about alien robots, super-powered mobsters, incorporeal assassins, or clouds of deadly green fire floating over Manhattan. They were both aware that, on the other side of this momentary escape, there would be dark days and trying times ahead. If Necrosis had been telling the truth, there was war on the horizon—a war that Tony would be called on to join.

On this night, though, Tony Stark and Pepper Potts found, however temporary, a moment of peace.

ACKNOWLEDGEMENTS

In the pages of *Iron Man: Mutually Assured Destruction*, Tony Stark ponders the cost of his sleepless nights spent creating . . . and, I have to admit, *many* sleepless nights went into the creation of this book. Amy, my fiancée—who is not altogether unlike Pepper Potts in her kindness, her wit, her heart, and certainly her ginger hair—was my rock during the writing process for this book. I remain grateful for her endless patience, her calming words, and her belief in my writing.

Here's the thing. I love Iron Man, and I believe that I really get Tony's passion, his heart, his heroism, and his drive as a person—but I am not the most tech-savvy writer in the game. Because of that, and so much more, I owe a debt of gratitude to Michael Melgaard, who guided me when I needed it most and championed this project from beginning to end. I can't say enough about Michael's work, as well as the work of everyone at Joe Books. From the editors I worked with earlier on other projects, to Paul Ruditis, who initially set up a meeting that got me my first gig at the company, I feel grateful to work with such a supporting and intelligent team.

I dedicated this book to my mother, who read to me from before I could understand the words, all the way until I was a teenager, holding back tears as we both read the conclusion to the final Harry Potter novel. My father would also tell me stories—he called them *Stories from the Mind*. I remember one where he retold the story of *Jaws* using the cast of *Teenage Mutant Ninja Turtles*. That was a favorite of mine.

All of my life, I have been given stories, and now, I get to give stories to anyone who decides to pick up this book. Tony Stark might roll his eyes at this . . . but that's a kind of magic, isn't it?

Pat Shand
November 2016